"You want to know what it's like to make love to me."

Jacquelyn would die rather than admit it, but silence was her confessor.

"And for a reason I still can't quite put my finger on, I am just as curious to know what it's like to make love to you."

"I'm trying to take that as a compliment," she said, rolling her head sensuously, as Nikos's grip loosened to a caress.

"You should. It's been a very long time since I felt anything like this. A very long time. Maybe never..."

He trailed a finger down her cheek. Her eyes fluttered closed, her lips parted. She felt the finger land on the cushion of her lower lip. She would not give in so easily. She would not grab him the way she wanted to.

Unable to sit still without reading, **Bella Frances** first found romantic fiction at the age of twelve, in between deadly dull knitting patterns and recipes in the pages of her grandmother's magazines. An obsession was born! But it wasn't until one long, hot summer, after completing her first degree in English literature, that she fell upon the legends that are Harlequin books. She has occasionally lifted her head out of them since to do a range of jobs, including barmaid, financial adviser and teacher, as well as to practice (but never perfect) the art of motherhood to two (almost grown-up) cherubs.

Bella lives a very energetic life in the UK but tries desperately to travel for pleasure at least once a month—strictly in the interests of research!

Catch up with her on her website at www.bellafrancesauthor.com.

Books by Bella Frances

Harlequin Presents

The Playboy of Argentina
The Consequence She Cannot Deny
The Tycoon's Shock Heir

Claimed by a Billionaire

The Argentinian's Virgin Conquest
The Italian's Vengeful Seduction

Visit the Author Profile page
at Harlequin.com for more titles.

Bella Frances

REDEEMED BY HER INNOCENCE

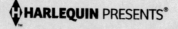

Recycling programs
for this product may
not exist in your area.

ISBN-13: 978-1-335-53866-6

Redeemed by Her Innocence

First North American publication 2019

Printed in U.S.A.

With grateful thanks to Joyce Young, By Storm, Glasgow and London for her insights into the world of wedding dress design

For Graham Frize,
Redeeming innocence wherever he goes.
Beautiful, sinful and wonderful friend.

CHAPTER ONE

Nikos Karellis walked straight into the bridal suite of Maybury Hall, Wedding Venue of the Year, and slung his suit carrier down on the four-poster bed. *So this is romance*, he thought, frowning at the frills and flowers and buckets of girly fizz. He lifted a bottle, checked the vintage and slipped it back into the watery ice. He was a long way off celebrating yet. He'd travelled through eight time zones and three continents, and he needed something a bit harder to take the edge off.

Finally he saw what he wanted, tucked underneath a gilt mirror featuring chuckling cherubs—a tray with decanter, glasses and water jug. Perfect. He poured a generous measure, then he added a little more, skipped the water, and sank it, the burn and peaty fumes soothing as they slid down his throat.

Cheers, Martin, he thought, tipping his glass at the chandelier. At least his former brother-in-law's taste in whisky was better than his taste in décor.

The bridal suite.

Of all the rooms in his flagship luxury hotel, Martin had chosen to put him up here. Maybe it was his idea of a joke, but it wasn't a very funny one. Pretty much nothing about being married to Maria made him laugh any more.

Nikos reached for the decanter, pausing in the act of pouring a second. The temptation was strong, but clear-headed was the only way to be tonight, because tonight was the beginning of the end, the face-to-face to get it all out in the open. Whatever it was that Martin thought had been hidden away in Maria's legacy, this was the night when they'd sort it out, because it was draining—and not just financially.

Despite what Martin's lawyers and the Inland Revenue seemed to think, there were no hidden assets, no secret stash of cash, no offshore investments. She had drunk them all, or snorted them all. And that was that. It would be a hard story to tell her doting brother, but Nikos was damned sure he wasn't going to leave anything out, because he'd had enough.

The tit-for-tat legal wrangling had gone on for too long so he'd done it the old-fashioned way; lifted the phone, and asked for a meeting.

When Martin suggested this black-tie event in one of his chain of luxury hotels, Nikos didn't hesitate. It was that or wait another six weeks until they'd even be on the same continent.

He could barely wait six more minutes now that he finally had the end in sight. Five years since Maria's death—but it was only his wedding ring he'd tossed into the cool, blue Aegean; the pain and the memories had been much harder to shift.

Too late to stop himself, he touched his ring finger. Empty space, smooth skin. Even though House, his high-end chain of department stores, was now in the *Forbes 100*, with turnover almost hitting the four billion mark, that feeling of bare skin felt better than anything. It was the feeling of freedom. More than that, it was the cast-iron knowledge that he was on his own now. On his own, forging his path, no wife hanging off his arm, or around his neck, no damage to clean up after—just these final few crumbs and then he really was home free.

He filled up a fresh glass with water and walked to the window. The estate was impressive, immense, expanding off into horizons of oak trees and lawns, and willow-draped lakes. He could just see the roof of the lodge house he'd passed and the huge iron gates at the end of the road, where a car had just pulled up. Something about it made him strain forward to see better...

But just then a knock sounded on the door, and he turned.

'I heard you'd arrived.'

Martin Lopez stood in the door and for a second they looked at each other. The same dark hair, dark eyes, sallow skin and high cheekbones as Maria—a look that he'd once found ravishing, irresistible, forging a love so strong he'd moved from delinquent eighteen-year-old biker to husband, in three years.

Looking back, which he had done all too often in the ten years they'd been together, it had been a predictable car crash of wrong place, wrong time. The minute he'd rescued her from the Bentley she'd wrapped around a lamp post on the side of the Sydney highway, they'd been inseparable—he was tennis coach, swimming coach, personal trainer, anything she could do to keep him in her life, and, after where he'd been, it had felt like arriving at the Promised Land.

Unfortunately some promises were very hard for Maria to keep.

'Martin. Good to see you.'

He walked towards him, stretching out a hand, reading in the light press of Martin's palm and the shifting of his gaze that he was on edge.

'Nikos. I'm glad you came. It's been a long time.'

'Too long,' said Nikos, holding the handshake a second longer, reassuring him that they were friends, no matter what had gone before.

'Yes, and I wanted to get in touch, but it's not been easy since Maria died.'

'I guess not. Our lives have taken different directions.'

'But we'll always have her in common.'

'I can't deny that,' said Nikos, staring hard at Martin, wondering what was really going on in his mind. He had done everything for the Lopez family; they were all set up for life. He had nothing left to give.

But something was eating the other man up. Martin dropped his gaze and turned back to the door.

'Shall I show you around, before the guests start to arrive?' he said, over his shoulder.

'Absolutely,' Nikos said, strolling out to the grand hallway, where the faces of various English rose aristocrats in grand gilt frames hung around the walls, no doubt wondering what the hell had happened to the old house now that the Lopez Hotel Group had transformed it.

'Yes, it's great to see you,' Martin said, stepping alongside him now like a best buddy. 'And I'm really grateful that you've agreed to present an award. We sold an extra fifty seats when it was announced yesterday.'

Nikos shrugged. 'It's no problem. I was on the way back from Sydney when I got the call.'

'Visiting your mother? How is she?'

They were at the top of a wide sweep of carpeted stairs, no doubt a prime photo opportunity for the hundreds of brides who used Maybury Hall.

'Ah, she's OK. Thanks for asking. She doesn't know me any more but she seems quite happy, and they look after her well.'

His monthly visits to Sydney were the one fixed item in his calendar. He knew they wouldn't last for ever...

'So how's business?' he asked, keen to change the subject.

They walked down the stairs, as staff carrying huge displays of flowers and cakes crisscrossed over the black-and-white floor beneath them.

'I'm getting out soon,' said Martin, with a mirthless laugh. 'This is the last sponsorship I'm doing. I want to end on a high. The hotels are doing well, but the wedding industry's being choked to death by overseas competition.'

'China?'

Martin nodded. 'It's hitting the dress side worst of all. With the volume they can produce overseas, there's just no profit margin for the little guy. Unless it's high-end, bespoke, but even then it's tough.'

'People will always want to get married,' said Nikos. People other than himself.

'Yes, but it's not what it was. Even the ones that have been on the go for years are feeling it. Another one of them is just about to hit the buffers, and it's one of my old pals who once owned it. It's his daughter's now.'

They rounded the corner of the staircase and fell into step walking on through the lobby. All around, the paraphernalia of an industry built on hormones and fiction—love and marriage. A sham that left Nikos stone cold.

'It's a pity, because she is a lovely girl—at least she was last time I saw her. But she's out of her depth.'

'As in overinvested, or out of her depth because she doesn't have the skill?'

'A bit of both probably. Which makes it awkward. She'll be here tonight and I've got a feeling she's going to make a pitch. And I don't have the heart to tell her she's the problem.'

'Yes, that's a tough one,' said Nikos, who had his own tough message to deliver to Martin, as soon as they got the chance to talk in private.

They turned the corner of the hall and stood on the threshold. Tables, heavy in white linen, spread off in all directions; the band at the side of the stage was tuning up a series of mis-matched sounds.

Soon the movers and shakers of the wedding world would all be here to congratulate them-selves on their achievements in this phony in-dustry, and he, the man least likely to marry ever again, would be presenting one of them with a cube of etched Perspex that would wind up displayed on a shelf somewhere. The irony wasn't lost on him.

Suddenly screens at either side of the stage flickered to life with images of Titian-haired brides in long flowing dresses running through fields of corn. That was it—he'd had enough.

'So what's the schedule?' he asked, folding his arms and facing Martin. 'Because we've got our own difficult conversation to have. And I want to make sure we've got enough time.'

'As soon as this is over. I promise you.'

'I'll wait until ten. We talk from then until this thing is finished. And then I'm leaving, Martin. And I won't be back.'

A shadow fell across Martin's face. His eyes darted furtively down and back up.

'I hear you,' he said, stepping closer. 'But it's not just me who's trying to get to the bottom of this. There are some people Maria was involved with that are very unhappy, Nikos. People that you know well.'

As if he'd felt a blow, Nikos flinched. Hair stood up on the back of his neck. Someone did a microphone check and a short burst of static screeched through the space.

'People that you know well.'

He'd thought this was all dead. Buried, with his wife. But it wasn't. It was still there, always there. Shadows that didn't fade in the warm afternoon sunshine or fresh summer mornings. Dreadful, dark shadows that never went away, no matter where he went or what he did.

'OK, Martin,' he said, dredging up his words, like hauling on armour. He stood tall, he breathed deep, he squared his shoulders. There was no option; there was never any option. But his mother was safe, so nothing else mattered.

He looked at the other man. It wasn't his fault. There was no one to blame but himself.

'We'll talk later,' he said. 'We'll get this sorted. They won't bother you.'

He patted Martin's shoulder as he passed, and made his way through the tables, scattered like giant confetti on the ground.

Two miles east of Maybury Hall, in the pretty market town of Lower Linton, Jacquelyn Jones, owner of Ariana Bridal, was also getting ready to attend the Wedding Awards, and with almost the same mix of dread and trepidation.

As designer-in-chief of the bridalwear boutique that had occupied the same spot on the main street for the past fifty years, she *could* have been going to collect an award. Her father had managed to do just that, scooping five top awards in the past two decades, but that was before she had taken over from him, and before the business had stopped turning such healthy profits.

No, she was going there tonight to get money. Or she was going to die trying. Because if she didn't, the whole thing was going to fall apart, one stitch at a time.

But first she had to get rid of Barbara, who had just slipped in through the courtyard garden as Jacquelyn had been closing up for the evening. With five husbands in the bag, she was the boutique's best, but also nosiest, customer. No doubt she had scented blood, or at least the high anxiety that Jacquelyn was trying to conquer as she arranged a vase of white arum lilies.

'So you're definitely going to the Wedding Awards at Maybury Hall tonight? Even though that snake-in-the-grass Tim Brinley will be there? Good for you! You go and show them all. It's disgraceful. He should be struck off, not getting a blooming award!'

'You can't be struck off for being unfaithful, Barbara,' said Jacquelyn, though goodness knew she would have done a lot worse to her ex-fiancé. 'And he deserves the award. He's a good photographer.'

'Tsk. You say that. But he owes everything to you and your connections. And it's not going to be easy on you though, no matter how hard you try to put on a brave face. After what he did! The thought of everyone whispering behind your back…'

'No one will be giving me a second's thought. Nikos Karellis is going to be there so they'll all be star-struck and googly-eyed over him.'

'What? Nikos Karellis, owner of all those House department stores? The billionaire Greek god who is now conveniently unattached?'

'I believe he's Greek Australian, actually,

though I really don't see the big attraction. He's not my cup of tea at all.'

'Oh, Jacquelyn,' said Barbara. 'You mustn't judge all men badly. Tim was cruel but there are plenty more fish in the sea and it's time you started looking.'

'This is an awards dinner, Barbara, not a singles bar.' She twisted a lily to the side, stood back to examine it.

'But Nikos Karellis—you might never get another chance! Think of the doors he could open for you! And you could do with some cheering up. You've not been yourself at all since Tim jilted you. It's affecting the business. Everything's got a bit shabby, if you don't mind me saying.'

Jacquelyn kept her face fixed on the lilies even though she couldn't see them, her eyes crushed closed in frustration and anger.

Barbara was right. She was completely right. And that it was so obvious was even worse. There was barely enough money to pay the machinists' wages let alone invest in a refresh of the boutique. And all avenues to borrow money had closed. The bank wanted the previous loan repaid and capturing the interest of a financier had seemed impossible.

She knew they cast her as a silly girl playing at shops, not as a serious businesswoman. She was caught in a vicious circle of stiff competition, poor profits and higher costs, and she couldn't seem to break free.

'I don't know what your parents were thinking disappearing off to the south of Spain, leaving you in charge here, after what happened. No wonder the place has run into difficulties.'

'Mum's rheumatics are what's taken them to Spain,' said Jacquelyn, 'and the last thing they need is worrying that they need to come back here. If you'll excuse me a moment...'

She stood up, scooped up the debris from the flowers and tossed it into the bin, then kept walking through into her studio, standing in the vale of light that flooded the space, desperate for a moment of calm.

But there was no escape, because right in front of her, spread out on her work desk, were the sketches she'd been poring over for the past two days. She swept them up, bundled them into a pile and bashed them off the top of the desk. They were rubbish. She knew they were, but she had lost all feel for designing fairy-tale dresses. She had lost her feel for fairy tales too. She needed practical things—like money—to hire someone who did.

'Oh, don't worry on that account,' called Barbara from the kitchen. 'I never mention a word about Ariana when I call. We keep it strictly social now. So much goes on in Lower Linton for such a tiny little town.'

And is regurgitated every Sunday on calls to Mum, thought Jacquelyn. Nothing went unnoticed or unreported. Nothing.

She looked up and saw Barbara position herself at the doorway.

'Barbara, it was lovely of you to drop by, but don't let me keep you. I'm sure you've got loads to do tonight.'

'Yes, I am rather busy,' said Barbara, narrowing her critical eyes as she wandered round the studio, like a detective in some third-rate TV show.

Jacquelyn wondered what clues she had left out and too late saw the piles of dirty teacups and balled-up handkerchiefs. Clues that might even find their way muttered into the hors-d'oeuvres of wherever Barbara dined tonight.

'Well, I hope you show that Tim Brinley what he's missing.'

Jacquelyn did her best to smile and tidied the scattered sketches into a pile. The inky sharp-limbed figure on top seemed to flinch as she was set down and Jacquelyn cursed the stress that was flowing through her, stress that was making it harder and harder to get these sketches right. And she had to get them right. She absolutely had to.

'I bet Nikos Karellis would happily help out. He's definitely got an eye for the ladies. If all else fails…' Barbara's voice trailed off as she raised a pencilled eyebrow and stared directly at Jacquelyn's figure.

'If "all else fails" what, Barbara? What are you trying to suggest? That I throw myself at a total stranger? Do you really think that's my style?'

Behind her, the row of mannequins looked on like a jury of headless Greek goddesses. She'd been baited and caught, exposing herself as easily as if she'd taken out an ad in the front page of the *Lower Linton Chronicle*.

'Darling, if it was your style you wouldn't be in this mess,' said Barbara as she lifted her clutch and re-formed her perfectly engineered face. 'And if I were you I'd start getting ready now. You're looking a bit puffy around the eyes. I'll see myself out.'

And she did, sailing past in a haze of sickly sweet scent, on through the studio to the hall-way, heels clicking on the stone steps and then out into the courtyard where they faded and were finally silenced by the dull thud of the wooden door.

Jacquelyn stood tight and tense until she finally heard the car roar off, then she let out a huge sigh and felt her eyes burn—again.

'Stop it, stop it. Pull yourself together!' she hissed through the hot self-pitying tears that had formed.

You knew this moment would come. Five years in charge and you let it all trickle through your fingers. Well, now it's happened. And you've got one chance left to stop this before it's too late.

She'd taken the once thriving family business and run it into the ground and had no one but herself to blame. She'd taken her eye off the ball, worried herself sick about things that turned out not to have been worth worrying about at all. Like a man. Like that stupid, stupid break-up, with that stupid, weak-willed man.

She sat down again, propped her elbows on the table and bowed her head.

Before her, the blank-faced sketches said nothing. She spread them out and stared at them. Any fool could see that there was something missing, something wrong. But she just didn't seem to know how to get them right. She'd whittled it down from twenty to twelve to this final bundle of six.

When she'd showed them to Victor, the pattern cutter, he'd been gracious and complimentary, but she'd known he'd been faking it. She'd seen the confusion in his eyes. Another dud collection. Again?

Around the studio, light was sinking into a pale mauve sunset. Through the window she could see traffic on the main road out of town that led to London. Just two miles east sat Maybury Hall, where the Wedding Awards were being held tonight.

She was running out of time. She had to get going. Everyone else could gush over Nikos Karellis, but it was Dad's friend Martin Lopez and his millions that she needed to see. She was going to approach him tonight and ask him to finance the business. She'd offer five per cent. Twenty per cent. Whatever it took.

Outside she heard a car prowl along the lane. Surely Barbara wasn't back again…?

She jumped up and ran out through the studio and down the stairs, then burst out into the courtyard. She slid the bolt across the wooden door and leaned back against it, breathing a deep sigh. But there was no knock, no screeching voice, just the quiet sounds and sights of a summer evening: water bubbling over the giggling cherubs in the fountain and the sun-dappled flower beds, sleepy and still.

Peace. If only she could stand still and enjoy it—but that was half her problem. Instead of busying herself out in the world, she had shut herself away, hiding in the familiar silks and satins, and beads and crystals that hung in the boutique.

She looked through the French doors of the shop.

Fairy tales were made real in there. Women were made into princesses. Dreams came true.

Once upon a time she'd believed that. She absolutely had. Happy ever after was the only ever after there was.

How wrong she'd been. Happy ever after didn't exist.

CHAPTER TWO

JACQUELYN STRETCHED HER SMILE and lifted a glass of champagne. She wouldn't drink it but it was the perfect accessory, and gave her something to do with her hands.

She might be feeling as if she were dying but she knew how to put on a show. Her dress was a fairy tale. How could it possibly be anything else? Her blonde hair was tousled, in a knot held up with beads of fine crystals, silken and soft and sparkling.

Her gown was cerulean-blue satin. The chiffon bodice crossed over her chest and the skirt billowed out in the signature 'Jones' cut that flattered and flowed to the floor. Her long neck and elegant shoulders were shown to perfection with a single pearl droplet on a fine chain. Her make-up was just the perfect blend of colours and tones to hide and highlight, and her lips were glossily, naturally, plump and soft.

All in all she was a walking miracle, she thought to herself. It was amazing what a few tricks of the trade could do. But if she, with her know-how and connections, couldn't make a silk purse out of a sow's ear tonight, who could?

She pulled her lips into a superhappy smile as a camera flashed a photo of the table, and all the while she surreptitiously scanned the crowd. She would not crack an inch in front of anyone, in case it got back to Mum and Dad. She was on show, wearing the most flattering cut and colour of dress.

'The best model you have is yourself,' as Dad always said.

'Don't you get too big for your boots,' said Mum.

Jacquelyn tried to straighten her shoulders, but they didn't need straightening. She twisted her head a tiny bit to the left, to see if Martin was here yet, but not so much as to be too obvious. Not that it mattered. They'd all think she was showing off to Tim Brinley or, worse, pitching for Nikos Karellis. As if.

She had been flippant, blasé, when Dad had phoned her about the awards.

Of course she'd be fine with Tim being there. Life moved on. And she would have a chat with Nikos Karellis if she got the chance, and, yes, she remembered his friend Martin Lopez. She promised she'd make a point of saying hello to him. She could give him a cast-iron guarantee on that front.

She felt the smile slip from her face and tension creep across her brow, and checked herself, taking a tiny sip of champagne and putting the glass down as if she were having the most marvellous evening, chatting and gossiping with the people at her table.

'I hear Nikos Karellis has arrived.'

'Made quite a splash already. In the bridal suite but with no bride, of course.'

'Ha-ha. I wonder who'll be the second Mrs Karellis.'

'I only just found out he was married to Maria Lopez. She was old enough to be his mother!'

'I don't think he's looking for a mother now!'

'I'd never heard of her before…'

'Where have you been? I thought everyone knew that story!'

Jacquelyn knew. She'd known the story for years, since the morning at breakfast her father had put the newspaper down with a, 'Good grief, you'll never guess who's died,' and then proceeded to tell them the story of his friend Martin Lopez and his beautiful sister, who'd married a man fifteen years younger. Photographs of him carrying her coffin, grief painted onto such a handsome face, had filled the nation's need for gossip for a day or so.

'Poor man,' her mother sighed, lifting the paper from her father's hands.

'Poor man, nothing. Rich man. He's worth a fortune now,' said her father.

'He's just lost his wife,' her mother chided. 'Money can't take away that pain, no matter what you say. He must have really loved her. Just look at him.'

Jacquelyn sipped her tea. She knew what love was. Every fibre of her being pulsed with it for Tim, her childhood sweetheart. Love was going to school with him, listening to music. He was her best friend, boyfriend and soon-to-be husband.

Love was them agreeing to save themselves for their wedding night, no matter how tempting, because there was nothing more important than that. Their secret pact, their complicit agreement. Their bond of trust.

There was no other option. Because that was what good girls did. Although it was never shown in public, Nonna Ariana was sniffy about the girls who wore white when they should be wearing ivory.

'If this is the most important day of their

life, then they should act like it. It isn't just a
fancy dress, it's real. They should know better,
bringing shame on their families!'

So Jacquelyn was steadfast. She was determined. And Tim was too, because it was all
going to be worth it. It was all leading to a rosy
future. It was the rest of their lives. What did
a few more months matter?

So no, Nikos Karellis had meant nothing to
her then.

And unlike every other woman here, he
meant nothing to her now. She wouldn't waste
a moment talking to someone whose interest
in women was superficial.

It was Martin Lopez she needed to find, and
fast. She couldn't bear it if this whole night
passed without a chance to give him her pitch.

'It's him. Here he is.'

She started, like a deer at the burst of a gun,
but it was just the hotshot Australian that had
entered.

'Wow, isn't he amazing?'

Despite herself, her head swivelled to the
front of the stage to see.

Well, physically—there was no doubt about
that. Was it the height of him, the breadth of
his shoulders, or the gleaming white shirt and
midnight-blue tux? Was it the short-cropped
dark hair and dark stubble, the trademark tat-

too that snaked from below his left ear and disappeared under the shirt collar?

Whatever, he was devilishly dark and handsome, and like every other woman in the room she found herself unable to stop staring. One by one, people crossed over to say hello, gushing and scraping before him— people that Jacquelyn knew to be supremely confident in business, acting star-struck and silly.

'Are you coming over to meet him?' said the woman next to her.

'No, thank you. I don't want to be caught in the crush of groupies,' she said, a little unkindly.

'Suit yourself,' said her companion, and stood up.

Jacquelyn turned to watch her shimmy her way across the floor, still trying desperately to catch a glimpse of Martin, but the crowd around Nikos Karellis was thick now and totally obscured the table.

And then she saw him seated beside Nikos. He was older than she remembered. Streaks of silver in his dark hair, but still a handsome man, and, she hoped, still a gentleman.

Her stomach turned a somersault and her hands dampened. She tried to wipe them on the tablecloth discreetly as she stood up.

Please, please, please *remember me*, she thought, and began to make her way across the floor towards him.

Nikos's patience had almost completely run dry. His smile was still fixed in place but he'd chatted and shaken hands with people all evening, in the bar and now here at the table. He hated the side effects of fame. The people who wanted to say hello were nice enough but they had no idea who he was—or where he'd come from. They were only seeing some airbrushed version of reality, as fake as the whole wedding industry itself.

He glanced down at Martin with a raised brow.

'How much more of this?' he said, leaning over.

Martin shrugged and smiled.

'The awards start in five minutes. After that we'll disappear off to my suite and talk properly.'

Nikos nodded and straightened up, trying to remember the name of the woman to his right who'd just introduced herself, but when he turned around, it wasn't a plump old lady who was right in front of him, it was a beautiful young woman.

She was tall, toned and blonde, and with a

practised sweep he took her all in—from the stunning cerulean-blue floor-length gown that held her feminine curves to perfection, and all the way up past the graceful curve of her shoulders, to the top of her elegant topknot.

She wasn't overtly sexual, but something about the shape of her hips and the neat swell of her breasts made his body react violently. And he noted with some pleasure that he hadn't felt such a reaction for a long time.

Suddenly the night was looking up, and even as he reached out his hand to shake hers, he made a mental calculation of how long he would be occupied with Martin before he could properly get to know her.

But she didn't take his hand.

She didn't even look in his direction. Instead she sailed right past him and stopped, as Martin looked up and got to his feet.

'Jacquelyn. It is you! I saw you coming across the floor and I wondered if it was. I thought I might see you tonight.'

Jacquelyn? Nikos quickly noted her name and watched, wondering how this exchange was going to play out. By the warmth in the way Martin was leaning towards her, lingering as he kissed each proffered cheek, he was clearly fond of her. But he had to be at least twice her age...

And the way she was holding herself was interesting: she was transmitting anxiety, with her spine so rigid, shoulders tense; and that smile, beaming a bit too bright.

'And this is my brother-in-law, Nikos Karellis. Nikos, Jacquelyn Jones—owner of Ariana Bridal. Her father Joseph and I were at school together.'

So, Martin really was old enough to be her father. That was helpful.

She turned her flawless face and keen blue eyes to Nikos. The smile she'd given Martin slipped slightly, he noted, and her spine tightened a notch more too. She blinked and with a long stretch of her arm she permitted her hand to be shaken.

Which he did and he read in that tense-fingered, quickly retracted handshake that he'd just been judged and dismissed. She didn't like him.

Well, it did happen. Not often, but he wasn't every woman's cup of tea. Particularly the ones who thought they were a bit above him. Even with all his money, he never forgot where he'd come from. And nor, it seemed, did they.

He knew the type. They saw his tattoos, his *warpaint* as his mother called it. The sensual ones saw brutality and found it fascinating.

The repressed ones didn't get him. They saw brutality and found it disgusting.

The truth, of course, was that he had left brutal back in Sydney at the side of the road. Bikers were brutal; his dad was brutal. His entire childhood had been brutalised beyond what any of these lovely people could understand. They had no idea that his mother suffered brain injury as a result of a beating from his father. Or that he had run drugs for him as an after-school chore.

The fact was that he'd made it his life's work to be free of every trace of violence and aggression. He'd severed ties with everyone except his mother, and poured millions into projects for delinquent kids.

So to be judged as 'less than' pressed his buttons, just a little.

He stood tall, squared his shoulders, one hand on his hip, in a gesture that called out her condescension.

'Former brother-in-law. My wife passed away five years ago.'

She dropped her gaze completely, and when she swept her perfectly oval lids open again there was a tiny flash of recognition.

'I'm sorry for your loss. I never met her but my father spoke about Maria. And you.'

Did he now? thought Nikos, his mind conjuring up an image of her baby blues widening over some story or other. Maria's high jinks were always being reported on some media space. And the look on her face told him that she was remembering something of that sort right now.

'Thank you,' he said. 'I appreciate your kind words. And I'm very pleased to meet you. Are you up for an award tonight?'

The dart of her eyes down to her feet and the blush of pink that bloomed over her face told him all he needed to know on that front. He was beginning to remember the earlier conversation. Was this the woman who was bad in business?

'No, I'm afraid not.'

'Someone else's turn, this year. But Ariana has won awards in the past, Jacquelyn, haven't you?' cut in Martin, gallantly.

'Oh, yes, one or two. We've won Wedding Dress of the Year and been runners-up a few times.'

'That's quite an achievement,' said Nikos. So the business was once at the top of its game. 'And is this one of your own designs?'

Despite her slightly dismissive glance he stood back to view.

He had a practised eye. He was a retail giant, for heaven's sake. House was the 'stylish woman's department store of choice', built on his keen eye, and in one of the most rapid, successful expansions in retail in recent years, he'd taken on concessions in all other departments. So he had every professional right to cast his critical eye over the very seductive shape of Ms Ariana Bridal, even as she tried to shield herself with her long slim arms, twisting to the side, speaking the least subtle body language he'd ever witnessed.

Then she started staring over his shoulder, as if looking for someone better to talk to, even more clearly communicating, *I'm not interested.*

Didn't she know that being not interested made her uniquely the most interesting person here?

'Sorry, did you say you designed this yourself?' he repeated quietly.

She turned, with a slightly irritated look on her face, which he found curiously seductive.

'Not me, but this is our original design.'

'Isn't this the Jones cut?' said Martin, whom Nikos was beginning to find more than mildly irritating himself.

'Nonna Ariana's, yes. Martin, I wonder if we might have a word,' she said, lowering her voice as she turned to him now and took a step away from the table. Martin mirrored her and moved away too. She was clearly trying to cut Nikos out of the conversation. 'Later on this evening? Would that be all right?'

Music started to play, people were taking their seats, Martin hesitated and Nikos raised his eyebrow, reminding him that he had a prior engagement.

'Tonight? Oh, I'm not sure. It's not ideal.'

'Please, Martin. There's something I want to discuss.'

The floor was emptying, people were taking their seats. They were beginning to look very conspicuous as the only three people still standing.

Jacquelyn knotted her fingers together as if she was praying. She looked truly anguished.

Martin looked at Nikos with a *what can I do?*

Nikos felt a tiny twinge of regret on her behalf but he had bigger things to worry about than a buttoned-up Englishwoman, no matter how attractive.

'Ah, this could be tricky. I've got Nikos here as my guest.'

She turned to look at Nikos as if he was even more of a pariah than she'd first thought, as if he were personally responsible for the fact that her business was dying on its feet.

'We'd better take our seats now. See you later, sweetheart,' he said, with a wink.

Jacquelyn walked back to her table as if she were entirely made of wood and tried to take her seat with grace that seemed to have completely deserted her.

Had she blown it already? She reached for her glass, something to hold as she quickly replayed the meeting in her head. Martin seemed to have been friendly enough but he'd been totally eclipsed by Nikos Karellis. And no wonder. The man was completely unnerving. She'd never met anyone so—*intense*. So physical. He'd made her self-conscious, tongue-tied and totally put her off her stride.

She slipped a glance to the side to look at him as the band struck up and was met with him staring right back at her. The hairs on the back of her neck stood up in an instant and she looked away.

All through the starter she could feel him staring and she absolutely would not look at him. Maybe he thought that she had gone over there to meet him? He probably thought that every woman was in love with him. He was so off the mark. She'd never let herself fall for a man like him. Anyway, she had one single mission here tonight, and it had nothing to do with love.

She turned again to tell him that with her eyes but he was talking intensely with the woman on his left. She watched as he listened to her, tilting his head towards her and smiling as the woman started flirting, throwing her head back when she laughed, playing with her hair, touching her chest and batting her eyelashes, all while Martin looked miserably at his salad.

She felt more and more desperate and in a haze of self-pity she began to cast around the room, looking for Tim. At the back of the hall she found him, his once boyish good looks now paunchy, his blonde hair thin.

He could have been her husband. They could have been sitting together at that table, waiting to collect awards, gossiping about how everyone was fawning over Nikos Karellis. At one point any other future would have been completely unimaginable.

Jacquelyn Jones not married to Tim Brinley? Don't be ridiculous—it's written in the stars...

But strangely enough she didn't feel wistful. And she didn't blame him for the mess of Ariana. She blamed herself. Funny how a crisis could put everything into perspective. And this was a crisis. For all she played it down with everyone, especially her parents, she was in a full-blown state of emergency.

She pushed the food about on her plate, unable to eat, and words seemed to stick in her mouth like cardboard. All she could focus on were the minutes ticking by and the location of Martin Lopez.

She sat through the tables being cleared, the lights being dimmed, and then the award hosts, two TV presenters she recognised from a breakfast show, arrived on stage to start the ceremony.

And then in a never-ending series of announcements and applause she sat through the awards, from Best Florist to Best Accessories, Best Cake to Best Make-Up, Best Venues to Best Stylist. When the Best Photographer names were called out, she prepared herself.

Suddenly there was the image of the winning photograph. A bride and groom on a horse. It was Tim's—it had to be. He loved to ride and he loved to use the riding motif in his photographs. It looked so phoney to her now.

The compère boomed out his name.

As the crowd burst with applause, she lifted her hands from her lap and tapped them together briefly. Most people wouldn't know what he'd done to her, but some of them would, and she couldn't let herself down by acting so childishly.

She forced herself to watch him accept his award, and she realised then that there was nothing there now other than the memory of a man she'd once loved, an outline of something once vivid. A bare-branched tree in winter, once so full of leaves.

She had so much more to worry about now.

The final award was Best Wedding Dress, and to announce it Nikos Karellis bounded athletically to the stage.

'He was her tennis coach,' she heard the woman beside her whisper.

'Ooh, he could coach me in anything he wanted,' said someone else, and giggled.

Jacquelyn tried not to roll her eyes, but she couldn't help looking closer, measuring his stature with her own innate sense of proportion. He was quite physically perfect. Exceptionally physically perfect. In the pit of her stomach something awoke, a swirl of longing, a primal feeling that tugged and shocked her, and she squirmed and moved in her seat. She looked around to see if anyone had noticed, but everyone's face was turned to the stage, eyes wide with interest.

The finalists were announced. The winning dress displayed on the screen and then the flushed and jubilant face of the designer, a pretty brunette. Nikos delivered the glass trophy, kissed her warmly on each cheek and gave her an affectionate squeeze.

Nice, thought Jacquelyn.

She had barely had a peck on the cheek in the three years since Tim. She was never the most physical person, but she liked affection, as much as everyone else. She liked being held close; she liked her hair being stroked and all the intimacy that came with being with someone you cared for.

Another wave of self-pity washed over her.

Was she destined to be single her whole life? Would she ever meet someone else?

She looked around the room. She might not be the youngest person here, but she was almost certainly the only one who was still a virgin.

She wondered if anyone knew. Sometimes she felt as if she were wearing a sign. And sometimes, there were moments she wished she could just go out and find someone and have sex and be done with it.

Those months after Tim left she'd tortured herself thinking she'd been wrong, stupid, blindly falling in with Nonna's views, not thinking for herself. She'd *almost* considered tracking him down to tell him she'd changed

her mind. But he'd gone. And that was that.
And now she was glad. She really was.

The ceremony was over. The audience was
applauding. The final comments were being
made. Some people had already started to
move. The lights came up. She spun back
round to see if Martin was still there, but he'd
gone.

She threw down her napkin and pushed back
her chair. It caught on the carpet. She struggled
to right it as she looked up. Where on earth had
he gone? Everyone was heading off to the bar,
but where was Martin?

Panic gripped her. What if she lost sight of
him? What if he disappeared and she couldn't
find him?

Then she saw him, heading off in the opposite direction. She picked up speed, almost
stumbling over the parquet dance floor in her
heels, desperate not to lose sight of him. But
then suddenly from nowhere Tim appeared!

'Jacquelyn, wait,' he called, and he reached
a hand around her arm.

She turned, confused, wondering what on
earth to say.

The days she'd spent longing for the tiniest
glimpse of him, five seconds of his time so that
they could 'work it out'. Yearning to see his

face, feel his hands, just be in the same room as him, again.

Now all she felt was embarrassment. All she could think was that he was holding her back from the one thing she had come here to do.

'I've got nothing to say to you,' she said, tugging her arm away. His face, the one she had once thought handsome, twisted as if she had slapped him.

'I know this isn't the right time,' he said, grabbing for her arm again, 'but you have to know that I'm really sorry about the way I treated you. I've grown up, I've moved on...'

'Look, I'm not interested.'

People were crowding at the opposite doors; thankfully no one seemed to be looking this direction. But he was right in front of her, blocking her view of the door to the hallway where Martin had disappeared.

'I thought I could do it but what you wanted was unnatural, Jacquelyn,' he whispered. 'I'm a man. I have needs and you wouldn't listen.'

'We made a promise!' she hissed. 'You never once said that you couldn't do it. Instead you just vanished! So you'll have to live with that. Now let me go, I'm in a hurry.'

'*You* made the promise for both of us. Your martyrdom is wasted, you know. That whole "pure as the driven snow" act is so last century.'

'Look, get out of my way. I couldn't care less what you think.'

She tried to step past him, but someone else was there.

'Is everything OK here?'

A deep Australian drawl, a strong unflinching presence.

'I'm trying to find Martin. Is he still here?' she asked desperately, smoothing her hair. The last thing she wanted was *him* to hear any of this.

Nikos's eyebrows were raised over dark eyes that flashed concern.

'I need to see him.'

'Yes, he's here,' he said, and he came towards her, reading the situation with a frown. Then he turned to Tim, bearing down on him with his six-foot stature.

'Don't you know any better than to crowd a woman?' he said, stepping further into the space, his body telegraphing masculinity, strength, power, the like of which she'd never experienced before.

Tim's face blanched and he took a step back.

'Now look here. I'm a friend of Jacquelyn's and I'm only trying to have a conversation.'

She looked at the two of them and a moment of clarity struck like a thunderbolt. Tim looked so short and plump and silly next to this man.

What on earth had she seen in him? She had wasted so much time and tears, and now she was reduced to begging for crumbs from some rich man's table when she should have been taking Ariana on to the next level?

She shook her head in despair. Where had she gone so badly wrong?

'Tim, the only reason you're here right now is because there are people here tonight who remember what you did, and you want me to say it's OK. Well, it's not OK. Nothing about it is OK. So why don't you take your half-baked little excuse for an apology and your stupid plastic award and get out of my way?'

She turned to Nikos, whose eyes were wide. She'd shocked him too. Good.

'I want to see Martin. Now. Where is he?' she said.

A grin broke out across his face and he stepped to the side.

'Come with me, I'll take you to him.'

CHAPTER THREE

MARTIN'S SUITE WAS in the Duchess Wing, about a mile of plush velvet carpet to the east of the grand ballroom. They walked in complete silence along its length until the ornate double doors came into sight.

Nikos had the good sense not to say a word until they got there but he was weighing up what he'd just heard and it sounded nasty. Whatever the guy had done, breaking a promise sounded like the least of it. And accusing her of being a martyr. Nikos had met more than a few of those, but in his experience they tended to be the nice ones.

Maria had never played the martyr. Maria took what she wanted and what other people wanted too…

'You all right?' he asked, his hand on the doorknob. 'Is there anything I can do?'

Jacquelyn looked up at him with eyes that told him she was still feeling some pain.

'I'm fine,' she replied. 'Thank you.'

Nikos nodded and opened the door of Martin's suite, ushering her in.

'I found your friend Jacquelyn. She wants a word.'

Martin looked up, surprised. He was sitting at a fireplace filled with yet another giant arrangement of flowers.

'Of course. If that's OK with you, Nikos?'

Nikos stood back and watched her sail right past him and perch on the sofa opposite Martin. Her back was ramrod straight and she turned, flashing Nikos a look that might have said, *thank you*, but might as easily have said, *beat it*.

'Yeah, sure. I was on my way to get my phone. I'll be back in five. That long enough, do you think?'

Martin nodded vigorously. Jacquelyn didn't move a muscle.

Nikos closed the door and walked back to his suite.

She was a force of nature, that one. The Ice Queen, but the way she'd blasted that guy was pure fire. It was impressive. And if she pitched like that to Martin he didn't stand a chance.

Maybe he'd been too harsh on her. She was clearly passionate about her business, and good for her. If he'd been in tough times, the last thing he'd want to do was waste his precious time on small talk with a stranger.

He collected his phone and checked for messages and emails, frowning when he saw yet another one from his accountant, Mark, about the investigation into Maria's missing assets. He had better get answers from Martin. This whole thing was getting more and more out of hand.

He rounded the corner of the hallway and paused. He put an ear to the door to see if they were still talking.

Martin's deep voice was making reassuring noises; Jacquelyn seemed to be silent. He knocked on the door and walked in.

'OK? All wrapped up?'

He didn't have time to worry if it wasn't. He had his own issues to deal with now.

'Nikos. Great timing.'

Martin was facing Jacquelyn. They were both standing, but now Martin was the one who looked imploringly at him, and Jacquelyn's eyes were bright with—hope?

'I was just explaining to Jacquelyn that I'm retiring. She's looking for an investor and I was trying to think of someone else who'd be a good fit. I don't know if I mentioned but Ariana Bridal goes back quite a long way. They need to modernise, perhaps? Would that be right, Jacquelyn? And so maybe you or your connections would be a...better fit...?'

Nikos shook his head.

'I'm not looking to invest in anything, Martin. I'm here to sort a problem.'

He held up his phone.

'A problem that's giving me a headache. While we were giving out awards, I've been getting more messages.'

'I won't take up much of your time, Mr Karellis.'

On a heartbeat Jacquelyn turned and walked towards him. She was breathtaking and he realised he was still standing holding his phone in the air. Quickly he pulled his arm down.

'Time is what I don't have. Martin?' he said, meaning, *Martin, what the hell are you thinking?*

'Maybe you could squeeze in five minutes with Jacquelyn before you go?'

'I promise it won't take longer than five minutes. Ten at the most. Martin understands. This is a business that has so much to offer. We go back decades and we've got great plans. We just need a break.'

Nikos looked at Martin, who raised his eyebrows and shrugged his shoulders as if to say *wouldn't hurt.*

With a sigh that he didn't even know he was going to make, he breathed out an, 'OK.'

'Five minutes. *If* we get this sorted,' he said to Martin. Then turning to Jacquelyn, 'Wait in the bar and I'll send someone.'

She nodded and smiled, and as she breezed past she stopped suddenly and grabbed his hand in both of hers. 'Thank you,' she whispered. 'I guarantee you won't regret it.'

He nodded gruffly, but the sensation of his coarse hand in her delicate fingers was sweet and soft and he was happy to linger there for a moment. He smiled, and she smiled back. Light seemed to sparkle in her eyes and her features lit up. The face of an angel.

She squeezed his hand and then let go and headed for the door, trailing behind her delicate scent.

He waited until she had gone and then closed the door. 'What the hell's going on, Martin?' he said. 'You know I'm under pressure here.'

'You could have said no,' said Martin, eyebrows raised.

'Garbage. You set me up. There's no way anyone could say no to that.'

'She's quite something, isn't she?'

'Hmmm,' said Nikos, 'but you do know that I won't be giving her anything other than some hard home truths? I'm not getting mixed up in anything. Especially with a woman who just needs to stand in a corner and whistle and she'll have men lying at her feet.'

'She's not like that at all. She's from a very good family.'

'That counts for nothing. Anyway, let's get on with this. What's going down? Why the year-long battle with your lawyers? Just what are you trying to prove?'

Martin stood with his back to the fireplace of flowers. The top of his greying head was visible in the ornate mirror. His face was cast in a sickly pallor, and he frowned and clasped his fingers. He was clearly agitated.

'I'm not trying to prove or disprove anything. My back's against the wall. All I know is that Maria had some investments. She was involved in something just before she died. I think it was illegal.'

Nikos nodded. No shocks so far...

'I see. Do we have any clue as to what it was?'

He noticed Martin wringing his hands again.

'Not exactly. She never confided in me—apart from the garbled message she left the night she died. And I think that's what the police are following up too.'

Nikos turned away. The night she died...almost the worst night of his life.

He'd turned up at his villa in Greece and found his wife topless in the hot tub with his old man. The night her drug-taking and his old man's drug-selling had combined in one fatal party. The night Nikos had walked away and never looked back, not even when she ran screaming after him.

No, he didn't ever want to think about that night again, but it didn't seem he had any choice.

'That stuff about the drugs?' he said quietly. 'We both know she bought them from my dad.'

'I think it's more than that. I think he's the one behind the other investments. At least, that's what he's telling me…'

Nikos looked up sharply.

'What do you mean?'

'I've had some communication from him.'

Suddenly Martin's sickly pallor and wringing hands made sense. Communicating with Arthur was never pleasant and Nikos had studiously avoided it for nearly twenty years. He blocked calls, emails, and every security guard knew his father's face on sight. He'd left Australia to get away from him, and he was damned if he was going to let him into his life in any way, shape or form ever again.

'OK. Out with it. What does he want?'

Martin cleared his throat.

'He wants forty million dollars. He says that that night they both went fifty-fifty on some investment she'd bought into in Cayman. He transferred five million dollars and then she… Well, you know what happened.'

'You don't really believe that, do you?'

Martin turned and leaned his hands on the fireplace.

'I don't know what to believe. He says he gave her the money and the company has qua-drupled in value. He says she invested it—and he works it out to be forty million that he says he's owed.'

'*Owed?*'

'By you as her beneficiary. And if you won't pay up—me.'

'He's insane. Did you tell him that she left nothing? Zero? That there is no estate—only trails of debt that lead in a hundred different directions. All I have is what I built myself and, trust me, I don't have a spare forty mil-lion lying around. I'd have noticed if I did. What evidence does he have for any of this?'

Martin shrugged.

'That's all I know. But I'm guessing you'll find out one way or another.'

Nikos laughed mirthlessly.

'I wouldn't give him forty cents, never mind forty million dollars. After what he did?'

He'd had enough of all this. He walked to the door, was there in three strides.

'Is that all you've got to say?' said Martin, still hooked around the fireplace.

Nikos turned. 'What else is there? He's a lowlife blackmailing piece of scum and if he thinks this is going to result in anything other than me hating him even more, he's mistaken.'

He opened the door and then closed it again.

'And I suggest you get yourself some better company to keep, Martin.'

He pulled the door closed and stood in the plush silent hallway, his heart thundering in his ears and his body primed for fight. He had to get a hold of himself or he'd rip someone's head off. He had to throw everything he had at it. But the fact that it was his old man who had stoked it all to life wasn't wasted on him. Everything he touched turned poisonous. Every goddamned time.

There would be some grain of truth in that cock-and-bull story because it was too crazy for there not to be. But he wasn't leaving it up to chance. He was going to go back to the villa and go through the vault. The one place he'd avoided for years might be the one place he'd find what he was looking for.

He speed-dialled his accountant.

'Mark,' he said, 'as soon as you get this I want you to check out every transfer that went into or out of Maria's accounts around the time she died. I'm looking for an investment in a company registered in the Cayman Islands. It's probably something that she'll have buried so it might be hard to find. That's all I have for now but I think this could be what's behind the investigation and the letters from Martin Lopez's solicitors.'

He clicked off the phone as a waiter walked past with a tray of drinks. Parties were still kicking off but he was in no mood to party. What he needed now was silence. And sleep.

He was jet-lagged and pumped with adrenalin, and there wasn't enough whisky in the whole place to knock him under. He needed to stand in a hot shower and hit the sack.

He pushed open the door of his suite, stepping out of his trousers, removing his jacket, heaving at his tie and unbuttoning his shirt with fingers that even now still shook with rage.

In the shower he stood, water from all angles pummelling his back and legs and head. He had to cool it. *Be cool. Rein it in, Nikos. Calm it.*

He thought of his mother lying in her bed in the nursing home. He thought of her sweet smile in the photograph of them at the beach, and then he thought of the blank, unseeing eyes that had looked at him the day before.

Every step he took was for her. To make her proud, to make all her own suffering worthwhile. He wasn't going to go under because of his father. He wasn't going to let Arthur ruin his reputation or his fortune. He was going to fight back.

He turned off the jets of water and dried himself. There was a noise outside. He opened the bathroom door a crack and listened. Someone was battering on the door. Martin?

He walked through the room, kicking up his suit trousers and catching them in his right hand as he opened the door with his left.

But it wasn't Martin. It was the blonde in the blue dress.

'Hi,' he said, confused. Then he slapped his forehead. 'Damn. Sorry. You've been waiting in the bar to see me. I said I'd send for you.'

Her eyes opened like starbursts, falling from his face to his chest and the towel knotted at his hips.

'Sorry, I was taking a shower.'

She stared at her feet, then down the hall, then at her feet. 'I am so sorry. I really did not mean to disturb you. It was getting so late… I'll go back and wait downstairs.'

'What time is it?' he said, trying to bury his impatience. This he could do without.

'Um…' she said. 'I'm sorry, I don't know. My phone ran out of power.'

'And I clearly don't have a watch on,' he said with a cynical chuckle.

She blushed furiously. She was very, very pretty when she blushed. She was very pretty, full stop. He could be in the mood to spend some time with her. That would be better than whisky at taking the edge off, for sure.

'Come in. I'll get some clothes on. We can chat now.'

He threw the door back and walked inside, tossing the trousers over a chair in the passing.

'If you don't mind, I'd rather not.'

He turned around, couldn't hide his surprise, but she was staring at her feet, her hands clasped in front of her.

'Much as I want to have a meeting with you, it wouldn't be appropriate for me to come in while you're undressed.'

He walked to the wardrobe and helped himself to a large white fluffy bathrobe, tied it at his waist.

'Suit yourself,' he said.

She looked up. Further along the hallway, noise bubbled out as a door opened. After-parties were probably taking place all over the hotel and she was too prudish to step over the threshold of his room?

'I hope you understand,' she said, taking another step back from the doorway. 'I want to talk about my business—that's all.'

He almost laughed out loud but when her face didn't break into a smile, he realised she was completely serious. How about that? She'd secured a meeting with him, but only on her terms. And those terms were...refreshing.

'Well, that's fine by me—but I won't be around for much longer if you still want that five minutes.'

'Maybe I could come by tomorrow morning before you leave?'

That would be a no, he thought.

With his flight scheduled for ten thirty, he'd be out of here an hour earlier, and the thought of cramming anything else into his head right now was not appealing at all.

But she looked so young, so full of hope. Like a flower opening its petals at the first burst of sunshine. He didn't really want to crush her, did he?

He nodded.

'OK. Come for breakfast. Nine.'

The sweet joy that spread across her face was beautiful, like a child's, and it was amazing how good that made him feel—for a second.

'Thank you so much. I promise not to waste your time.'

'We'll see,' he said.

But as he put his hand on the door and began to close it, his phone lit up. Mark. More bad news.

CHAPTER FOUR

A SLEEPLESS NIGHT, anxiety and a heatwave. What a killer combo. But at least she had a reason, and a fast-approaching deadline.

Jacquelyn flew around the studio tidying up the mess she'd made over the previous four hours. She was exhausted but she was getting ready to meet Nikos Karellis and for the first time in ages she felt hopeful, optimistic— happy?

It wasn't what she'd set out to do, but it was even better than finance from Martin Lopez. This was a chance with House, for goodness' sake! It was the retail sensation that had expanded when everyone else was shutting up shop and disappearing down online rabbit holes.

Just those four brief meetings with Nikos Karellis had lit something up inside her, ignited some hunger that she'd never possessed before. Something had rubbed off and made her want to be part of that world. It was as if he'd sprinkled some of his magic dust and she'd breathed it in, and from the moment she'd closed the door to his suite, she'd been unable to get him out of her mind.

Who are you trying to kid? she thought fleetingly. *You saw him nearly naked and you're as hooked as every other woman. The only difference is that you were afraid to step through the doors to see where it might lead. But you could have...*

No. This drive to get it right had nothing to do with any attraction to him as a *man*. She would never dream of having a business meeting in his suite. This was all about Ariana. It was so important to get it right!

And she would. She'd tossed and turned for a couple of hours, got up at three and then started work. By six she had completely re-worked the strategy. She'd created four personas of Ariana Bridal clients. She'd sketched out a cost-benefit analysis, which presupposed cash injection from House. And then she'd gone the extra mile and thrown in some figures based on the concession opportunities that she'd gain linked to the brand. It was all pure speculation and she could be way, way off, but it showed imagination. It showed that she'd done some homework at least.

So she still hadn't fixed the designs. But that part would come. With cash they could hire a designer again, someone who could really capture what it meant to be an Ariana bride...

She practised her pitch out loud as she poured her fourth coffee and walked with it through to her bedroom to start getting ready. She would show him what she was capable of. She wasn't some airhead underachiever; she was the heart and soul of this business, and with his cash injection Ariana could be a great little addition to his portfolio.

But first she'd need to make a start on her appearance.

The clock showed seven. Just under two hours should be fine. She'd have time for a quick face masque and then some brightening cream. Then she'd plaster on the concealer and some coral lipstick.

She heard the door and tried to peer outside. There was a huge black car in the lane. Barbara, in one of her current husband's limousines. She'd be 'on her way to the gym', which really meant she'd been scouring social media since she woke and couldn't wait to get the details. She probably already knew about her breakfast meeting with Nikos.

'Hello, Barbara,' Jacquelyn said, as brightly

as she could, as she pulled back the bolt on the door. 'This is an early call today.'

'Hello, Jacquelyn.'

Nikos!

He looked fresh and vital in a crisp white shirt and dark jeans, but with that solar intensity that made her take a step back. Her hands flew up to her hair in a defensive motion as she did a mental checklist. Three hours' sleep, four hours' staring at a screen, four coffees, no make-up, hair everywhere. She stared down— a skimpy camisole and pyjama shorts.

'What are you doing here? How did you know where I lived?'

'I looked it up,' he said simply.

'But I thought I was to come to Maybury Hall at nine. Isn't that what you said? Oh, no, I've not messed this up completely, have I? I've been working on a presentation all morning. I've personalised it just for you. And House.'

'No, it's not nine,' he said with a wry laugh. 'It's only seven. And I've come by here on my way to the airport. Something's come up and I've got business to attend to I can't put off.'

He was solemn, sullen and serious. He was going and taking with him the air that she needed to breathe. She felt bereft—as if the ray of hope, the hot air balloon that she had finally found to take her over this rocky ground had just been punctured. All those hours she'd spent she'd completely convinced herself that there was no way forward now other than with concessions in the House stores.

'We can reschedule?'

Reschedule? She knew a brush-off when she heard one.

'Oh. I see.'

She knew by the slight surprise in his eyes that she hadn't hidden her disappointment at all well. But this was awful. This was the pacifier that Martin Lopez had passed her. There was nothing else.

'I'm sorry—I realise that you are a very busy man. I hope everything is OK.'

'Everything will be OK, thanks. And I'm perfectly serious about another time. My assistant will be in touch in a couple of days to sort out a date...'

She hesitated, the words of despair held back in her mouth. *When?* she wanted to whine. *Because in six days we could be closed down... gone...forgotten.*

'Oh, that would be wonderful. If you have the time.'

'Of course. It would be my pleasure.'

He looked so sincere, and seemed to hesitate when she extended her hand, put on her smile.

'Well, thank you anyway. It was lovely to meet you last night, and I'm very grateful for your time. I do realise how busy you are.'

He looked away. 'I'm a man of my word, Jacquelyn. I said I would listen to your pitch and I will.'

She heard the words but her disappointment seemed to know no bounds. It was the light going out. It was exhaustion. It was being up all night and so full of adrenalin.

'Please, don't worry about it,' she said, on a sigh.

'Look, I'm heading to Greece. Why don't you come along on the flight—make the pitch then? I often have meetings as I travel; if you're OK with that, I'd be happy to accommodate it.'

Travel with him on his plane? Alone? To talk about Ariana and House. That was intense. Insane. That was the offer of a lifetime.

'Why yes, that would be super,' she said, her mind running ahead, but then… 'When do you fly?'

'I'm on my way to the airport now.'

'Now? As in right now?'

She looked down again at her skimpy clothes and then up into his face, which seemed to have softened slightly.

'Don't worry. I won't ask you to pitch in

your pyjamas. The flight will take a few hours. I'm going to be busy for a while—you can finish your presentation, if that's what you want to do. There should still be plenty of time for the pitch. If there's not enough time, do it after lunch. You can come to the villa. Fly home later this evening. You'll be back at work tomorrow.'

He stepped out into the street and seemed to look over his shoulder.

'OK? It's the best I can do.'

'I'll take it,' she said, knowing that this was in fact a better offer than she could ever have imagined. Travelling with Nikos to his villa in Greece. Lunch and then making her pitch. Surely this indicated that he was really interested in what she had to offer?

'Could you give me ten minutes?'

He checked his watch; he raised his eyebrows.

'Five?' she said.

He nodded and stepped inside.

'I'll be right back.'

With an energy she didn't know she possessed Jacquelyn flew upstairs to the flat, ran a shower and was in and out of it in under a minute. She dragged a brush through her damp hair and tied it into a braid. She lathered cream on her face, hands and arms and threw her favourite cornflower-blue sundress over her head. With a minute to spare she applied deep pink lipstick, slid on gold jewellery and leather sandals.

Never in her life had she gotten ready so fast. She looked flushed and desperate, but the light golden tan and blue of the dress picking out the blue of her eyes made the whole appearance somehow alive.

Let that be a lesson, Jacquelyn Jones, she thought.

She tossed a jersey dress into her bag and clean underwear, just in case, then grabbed her laptop, the folio of designs and looked around the studio. Coffee cups, handkerchiefs and the half-eaten slice of toast she had started and then discarded.

She ran downstairs, pulled the door closed and went out into the courtyard where Nikos was waiting. He stood in profile, staring at the fountain, lost in thought.

She beamed at him, carried away by her own enthusiasm and energy, but when he turned to look it was with a face etched deep with concern.

'Is everything OK?' she asked, suddenly stalling on the steps.

He focused on her, swept her with his eyes and then his face seemed to brighten.

He put his phone in his pocket.

'Yeah,' he said. 'Sure. All good. You look beautiful, Jacquelyn.'

'Thanks,' she said, astonished. Because getting a compliment from a man like him seemed to be worth more than getting a compliment from anyone else. It didn't make her flesh crawl or make her feel patronised. And she wanted him to think she was beautiful.

How odd that she should care...

He smiled.

'Let's go to Greece,' he said.

CHAPTER FIVE

SO HE DIDN'T always make the right decisions, and extending a pity invitation to Jacquelyn Jones was definitely not one of his best. As soon as he'd taken the second call from Mark, he should have followed his first instincts and sent her a message.

But when he'd found out that Ariana Bridal was only two miles from Maybury Hall he didn't have the heart to drive by. And all he was going to do was offer her another place, another time, and, if he was completely honest, hopefully another agenda—one not related to business.

With every passing minute he had regretted this gut reaction to those blue eyes. He owed her nothing but somehow he'd found himself agreeing to meeting her not once but twice. This was getting way out of hand.

They'd had no time to talk on the flight—he could have predicted that—and the time of this pitch had dragged on now, to some post-lunch rendezvous, every minute heightening her optimism and dimming his.

But in a way it had been a salvation having her chatting away and oohing and ah-ing about the scenery on this first journey back from the airstrip to the villa. He doubted she'd noticed him turn his head away when they neared the hairpin bend that dropped to the steep olive grove where Maria's car had taken its tragic turn.

The skid marks were still on the road, twin black lines, baked into the cement. On through the village of Agios Stephanos they drove—it was almost exactly as he remembered, the bakers, the store, the old men who stared, and dogs tied up in pockets of shade, barking at the cars as they passed.

He pointed out the tiny old white church clinging to the side of the steep cliff, rough-ened with centuries of hot sun and windswept winters. His great-grandparents had been mar-ried there, and their parents and grandparents before them, but he kept those facts to himself.

Further on, faded signs sent far-travelling tourists to sacred wells, and a stream trickled down to the level of the sea, where his private shingle beach presented itself to crystal-clear aquamarine waters, and where once upon a time he'd moored his boat.

Once upon a time this had been the one place on earth he'd felt truly alive, and truly alone. It was in his DNA and it was a thousand miles from Sydney.

Maria hadn't particularly liked it here—too basic, too boring—and he'd seen no reason to try to change her mind. He'd kept it private and personal, loving his times alone here. Occasionally he'd entertained like-minded clients who'd turned into friends, but never, it had to be said, anyone who was still at the stage of pitching a proposal.

He stood now in the library, sheaves of papers strewn all over the table. Beyond them, through the window, he looked out over the old familiar gardens and tennis courts, down to the pool house to where, with another apology, he'd sent word for her to wait for him.

The hour he'd asked her to wait had become three, as he'd rummaged through Maria's unfiled documents, with calls back and forth to Mark. He'd sent more apologies and the offer of anything his guest's heart desired, including food and drink, spa treatments from his private masseuse and her choice of clothes from the vast wardrobes in the villa.

Finally, he closed the door of the safe, clutching the bundle of papers that he'd been searching for. They were a mess but they showed Maria's ownership of a company listed in Cayman. He connected by video phone to Mark and his lawyer and together they went through them word by word. It seemed that she'd bought a shadow company, but that it had ceased trading six months later.

There was no sign of any money ever changing hands between her and his father. And there was no sign of any profits, which meant that neither his father nor Martin nor the Inland Revenue were due anything at all.

Finally even the calm, unflappable Mark breathed out a sigh of relief. And that said something.

'That was a close call. I don't think we're out of the woods yet, but at least we know there was stuff happening that you weren't party to. This is good news.'

Good news. He nodded as the knowledge sank in. His wife had deceived him in new and even more dangerous ways. It shouldn't really have been a surprise, but it was still painful. And what else was he going to find out?

'I take it you'll be out of commission for the next few hours in some kind of post-apocalyptic celebration?'

'For your information, I'm going straight

into another meeting. I've got someone wait-ing to pitch a new concession for House.'

'A pitch? On Sunday. After what you've just been through?'

'It's no big deal. I don't think it'll come to anything. It's a favour to a friend—it's bridal-wear, bespoke—not something I see working for us. It's not the right brand, but I might be able to give her some feedback that'll help.'

'Sounds like just the way to unwind after averting an unaffordable tax bill, a rush on your stock and a media storm. But hey, who am I to judge?'

Nikos raised his eyebrow at Mark's attempt at humour. He was emotionally wrung out, stressed out and jet-lagged. And now he had this to do. Mark was right. He wouldn't be able to focus on a word she was saying. He had to just chill for a couple of hours.

'Incidentally, I've doubled your security in the short term. Until all this blows over. I think it's best to be on the safe side.'

'Is there anyone here in Greece?'

'Not since after the break-in. Your last-minute change of plans caught us off guard but I can get a couple of guys there if you want.'

'It's OK, I'll be heading back soon. Thanks,' said Nikos, then clicked off the phone and pocketed it. The break-in six months earlier had taken him by surprise, but it was just some opportunistic petty criminal. They'd been disturbed before they could take anything.

Still, he was glad Mark had the sense to step things up. He'd felt uneasy leaving Manhattan, but then, these days he felt uneasy everywhere. Leaving Maybury Hall he'd felt something wasn't right, that strange car, parked too long, that just happened to stop off at Lower Linton when he did…?

He was probably getting paranoid.

He tripped down the steps to the pool, just as he caught sight of Jacquelyn, sitting under a parasol in the shade, her laptop in front of her, staring intently at the screen. Her brow was furrowed and her eyes intense, her lips moving, her hands gesticulating—she was practising her pitch to him.

Oh, man. She was all geared up and he was gearing down.

He took the last flight of steps, slowing his pace, trying to think of the best words to begin his own pitch to her. He knew his own body—he was buzzed up and he needed release. It was either sex or exercise. It wasn't politely listening to a friend of a friend telling him about her plans to bring more fishtail wedding dresses to market.

He strode past the drained hot tub, ignoring

it, and right up to the pool house, just as she noticed him. She looked up, startled, touched her hand to her chest in an endearing way. In her simple blue sundress, with broad straps over sleek shoulders, she looked good. She looked great. That was all he could think.

'I'm so sorry!' she said. 'I didn't see you there. I would have been ready for you up at the house if I'd known.'

'I'm the one who needs to apologise, dragging you all this way and then leaving you here to fend for yourself all afternoon. Have you been OK? Got everything you need?'

'Yes. Totally,' she said. 'I've had a lovely afternoon sitting out here. It's the best waiting room I've ever been in. It's beautiful. You're so lucky.'

He looked around, nodding. The Aegean was particularly calm, particularly blue. Behind him sparrows were flying in and out of the bushes and hedges that screened the pool, just as they'd always done. The sun was beginning its late afternoon slide, the light that perfect hot, bright dazzle that made everything look at its best. And the pure, cool twenty metres of water right beside him looked as inviting as he'd ever seen it. It was pretty near as perfect as anywhere could be.

Jacquelyn stood up and smoothed her dress,

catching his eye. He forced his gaze to remain on her face.

'So where do you want to do this?' she said brightly. 'Up in the house? It's only me and the laptop. I can fall in with whatever suits.'

He ran his hands through his hair, biting down on the adrenalin that was building in him. He didn't want to go back in there. He didn't want to sit down politely and listen to anything she had to say. He wanted to be out here, in the sunshine, living life, remembering Greece the way it used to be for him. He wanted to shake off the cobwebs of Maria's death once and for all, and he couldn't think of a more engaging woman to do it with.

'To tell you the truth, the thing that would suit me most now is just to chill for a while. I've been on the go for hours and I need to unwind.'

He glanced at the pool house and her eyes followed his, widening when she looked back at him.

'How about we shelve the business talks for a bit? I don't think that tagging on a pitch right now is going to be the best idea—we both need to be clear-headed. What do you say?'

He winced as the words came out of his mouth. She was going to be more and more convinced that there was a crock of gold at the end of this rainbow when, really, it was much more likely to be a crock of something else.

'Well, yes. Of course. I don't want to get in the way. I'll fall in with your plans. You were good enough to invite me here in the first place—I'm just happy to get the chance.'

Why did that irritate him slightly? That she was glad only to be here for her five-minute pitch? He wanted her to want to be here because he was Nikos Karellis the man, not the CEO of House. He opened a bottle of water and splashed some into two glasses, handing her one.

'You need to stop apologising for yourself. Would be my first piece of business advice. If what you've got to offer is worthwhile, people will be prepared to wait for it.'

Her lips formed a surprised 'oh' and he was sure she was about to start with another apology but she clamped her mouth closed.

'Thanks for the advice, then,' she said, taking the glass and putting it straight down on the table.

'You're welcome. Always better to say thanks for your patience than to apologise for holding someone up. It's assertive. Someone in your position needs to be very assertive.'

'I've never had any complaints before,' she said, and he noted as she drew herself up. He

noted because the slight movement drew his
eyes to the curves under her dress, the way it
creased and hugged and flattered.

'I'm sure you haven't had many complaints
at all,' he said, and he meant it innocently
enough, but in the pause that extended now
between them, in the moment in which they
each regarded the other, the unmistakeable
heat of sexual tension began to bloom. He felt
the physical rush and saw it reflected in the
widening of her eyes, the slight parting of her
lips.

'If any,' he finished, underlining the point,
unnecessarily.

'I meant,' she said, clearing her throat, 'I
haven't had any complaints about being assertive. Though that doesn't seem to get me
anywhere. In the business world.'

He drained his glass and reached for more.
In the quiet afternoon, the only sounds were
the slosh of water in his glass, and the bursts of
cicadas through the heavy heat. The sun beat
down on his back, warmth spread and seemed
to soothe his tense shoulders. The world was
beginning to slow and right itself. Greece was
seeping under his skin again.

'Maybe you've been talking to the wrong
people. I guess some people, some men, are
threatened by an assertive woman.'

'Well, I can't seem to be any other way,' she said, walking to the edge of the terrace. She placed her hands lightly on the top of the barrier and stared out to sea. Sunlight glinted on her golden hair and bathed the edges of her shoulders; the skirt of her dress floated up in the warm summer's breeze.

'Be yourself,' he said. 'It's working well from where I'm standing.'

She cast a glance back over her shoulder.

'With all due respect, it's easy for you to say. You don't have to ask anyone to finance your company. You've got everything you could ever need.'

Everything he could ever need? People thought that having the cars and houses and planes was everything. Easy mistake to make but they were so wrong. He wanted peace. He wanted trust. He wanted to be able to wake up in the morning to birdsong; he wanted to roll over in his bed and hold the warm body of the woman he loved, not slide into cold space, wondering where she was and who she was with, and what she'd done.

But he doubted he would ever find it, if it even existed.

'I'm sorry,' she said, and he looked up from his self-pity. 'I overstepped the mark there. I had no right to say that. It was unprofessional.

I just want you to know that I'm really grateful for this chance—I don't want to do anything to ruin it.'

'Oh, come on, Jacquelyn. Give yourself a break. Maybe you should try being a bit less professional for a while. All I'm saying is that I'd be grateful for your company for the next few hours. As one human being to another, the real Nikos and the real Jacquelyn.'

She was on the back foot. He could see tension in her eyes and the nervous way she clasped her hands. She walked over to where her laptop sat and moved it out of the wedge of sunlight that had crept onto the table. Then she closed the lid halfway.

'Well, the thought of spending time here... Who wouldn't want to do that? I mean, it's gorgeous, and I haven't had a holiday in four years, but...'

'There's a "but"?'

'But can I get your word that the pitch will definitely go ahead?' she said, her hands clasped in front of her chest.

'The pitch will definitely go ahead,' he repeated, nodding. 'Come hell or high water, you'll get your chance to talk about your business. I'm only talking a walk, a swim, then an early dinner. You could stay here tonight— there's plenty of space,' he said quickly, when he saw a look of surprise and shock sweep over her face. 'Get an early night and then you'll be fresh for the morning. Pitch at nine and I'll have the jet ready for ten-thirty. I'm heading back to New York via London tomorrow too. I think that would work—yeah?'

'You mean stay all night? I don't think so. I wasn't really counting on that. I'm not really prepared.'

'I wasn't counting on it either,' he said, with an honesty that he didn't expect. 'This is the first time I've been back here in years. I thought I'd hate it, I thought I'd want to get away the minute I…found what I was looking for in the vault, but I don't. I really want to hang out, relax.'

He looked round again at the terrace, the pool, the bushes popping with colour and even the empty hot tub that shimmered in the baking heat. The olive groves behind him on the hillside, the goats roaming free. This was home, and he'd had no idea how much he'd missed it.

'Come on. If you won't do it for me, do it for the staff who're slaving in that kitchen preparing dinner for us tonight. You can't let them down.'

'That's not fair. That's blackmail,' she said, but a smile was tugging at her lips.

'I never said it was fair. But if you want that on your conscience…'

'OK. I'll stay. As long as I can get an early night in the guest bedroom…'

'Of course. That's a given. So on that basis we have a deal?' He laughed, and extended his hand.

'Deal,' she said, and as she slid her hand into his, and looked up with those cool blue eyes, he knew there was a fire that burned there, and he was even more sure that there was nothing he wanted more on this earth than to light it.

CHAPTER SIX

THE BRIGHT AFTERNOON sparkled and finally faded as the lilac clouds of dusk slipped through purples and mauves and came to settle over the low hills. Night wrapped warm arms around the vast lands of the villa, snuffing out everything except the sconces on the walls, the lamps dotted on paths and the fiery glow of the man himself.

Jacquelyn, freshly showered, hair long and loose, slipped into her silk jersey maxi dress and stepped out on the terrace to watch.

Her hands curled round the cool metal barrier and she breathed, deeply. What a day. From the moment the plane had touched down on the soil she'd been swept up in love for this place. The light, the scents and sounds, every fabulous aspect of this fabulous villa. And then spending the last part of the afternoon walking through shady olive groves, visiting the fabled Well of Agamemnon and sitting on Nikos's private beach.

She could hardly believe she was the same person who had been so dismissive of Nikos Karellis only one day earlier. Now her heart raced and her stomach fluttered at the thought of his face breaking into a smile, as he took her hand to guide her down the worn sandstone steps onto the baking sand.

She'd been right not to strip off and swim though, tempted as she was. But that would have been a step too far. Instead she'd kept her sundress on and her dignity intact, and watched happily from the tiny terrace as he'd emerged from the pool house in a pair of swim shorts and jogged past her into the sea.

He was magnificent. All that she'd denied herself in that flash as he'd opened the door to his suite, she'd then feasted on from the safety of her deck chair. She'd gorged herself on the rippling muscles of his back, his firm calves and thighs as he'd pounded past her to the waves. The sight of his fabled tattoos winding from his neck over his back and his chest, tracing their silky path over strong, hard, perfect muscles.

He'd pounded the waves, swimming out some fifty metres and back, making her feel stupidly, ridiculously nervous when he'd almost seemed to disappear in the foaming white horses.

And then finally he'd emerged and walked towards her, dragging a towel this way and that, mesmerising her, like a magnificent god-like hypnotist. She'd been powerless to stop herself. And that was OK. Because all she'd been doing was looking. And as long as she remembered that, she was in no danger.

But even now as she stood watching him on the terrace below, she knew that every single thing about Nikos Karellis eclipsed every single thing about every other man she'd ever met. Back and forward he paced, like a general pacing in front of his army. In the calm, silent night his voice carried to where she stood, switching from the Greek she barely recognised, to Italian and then back to his deep, drawling Australian English—he was orator, statesman and king all in one.

She knew she should be thinking about her presentation, but she simply couldn't make her mind focus. Yet. As long as she had an early night, she'd be up at dawn and get back into the zone.

'Hey up there! Juliet! Coming to join me?' said Nikos. He had walked to the end of the terrace and was almost underneath her.

'Yes, Romeo, just coming,' she laughed. She lifted her fingers to her lips to blow him a kiss, and then stopped—what was she thinking? She drew her hand back as if she had been intending to tuck her hair behind her ear.

But the look in his eyes told her he knew. He knew she was attracted to him. She was useless at hiding it. From the way she'd drooled as he'd dried himself down, to the way she'd been caught, open-mouthed, watching him just now.

Of course she was attracted; who wouldn't be? The question was, what was she going to do about it?

She slipped silently along the hallway, her feet slipping on the marble, her silver bracelets jangling. She caught sight of herself in the mirrored doors that led out to the terrace.

You'd better be careful, Jacquelyn, she told herself. *You're almost out of your depth. Don't spoil it all now...*

She walked across the lamp-lit terrace. Nikos walked towards her, and her heart leaped in her chest. She breathed, she smiled. She took the cheek he offered, right, then left, and she kissed him quickly, ignoring the swirl of musky male scent and the smooth warmth of his skin.

'You look very beautiful,' he said. 'That coral colour suits you. The cut of the dress—really nice.'

She knew it did. The soft jersey draped over her figure, hugging her curves, the coral pink toned with her skin. She was lucky.

'Thank you,' she replied as he showed her to her seat at a round table, tucked in the corner of the trailing rose arbour, lit by candles and strings of little lamps.

'Are you hungry?' he asked as he settled himself beside her and speared a bit of melon, watching her carefully.

'Oh, yes,' she said, looking at the plates of appetisers. But she wasn't. She wasn't hungry in the slightest.

He nodded, still watching, and she lifted some food to her plate.

'Your room OK?'

'Oh, yes. Thanks. Very comfortable.'

He nodded. 'I've been busy, but that swim did me the world of good. Unfortunately it was all waiting for me when we got back from the beach.'

'I guess you're always on call.'

'Aren't you? As head of a business, there never seems to be a moment when someone doesn't want an instant solution to some problem or other.'

'I'm not quite in your league. My issues are more around being taken seriously.'

He raised a sharp eyebrow.

'Not by my staff. But by men. Bank managers usually.'

'You feel objectified in the business world?'

'Objectified. Patronised. Demoralised. Take your pick. I'm sorry if I sound bitter, but the number of times I've heard *"Oh, isn't your father coming?"* Honestly. It would never happen if I were a man.'

'People make judgements in less than a second. It takes a lot to change a preconceived idea, but I bet you can do it if you want to.'

It was the thing that upset her more than anything else. Taking over from her father, and feeling that sense of disappointment every time it was she alone who walked into meetings. It was fine when she was just there as window dressing, but as soon as she was running the whole show she knew she'd been judged and filed before some of them had even read past the first line of her accounts.

'I don't imagine anyone has ever told you you're far too handsome to be getting all mixed up in business before?'

'No,' he said, scathingly. 'And I honestly can't believe in this day and age that anyone would doubt your credentials because you're a woman.'

'It happens,' she said, taking a sip of wine, feeling it slide warmly into her stomach.

'If it's any consolation, you wouldn't begin to imagine what's been said to me. The question is, do we let what other people think affect our decisions?'

'Is this about to turn into my second piece of business advice?' she asked, smiling as she took another little sip of the very delicious wine.

'Life advice,' he countered.

'So why exactly does Mister Seventy-Sixth-on-the-*Forbes*-List feel so maligned?'

'I don't. But what I'm trying to get across is that people paint pictures in business. And in life. The perfect world you think you see here…'

He jerked his fork around the space. Lamps were now glowing softly right along the lines of the terrace, highlighting clumps of sleeping flowers nestled in their bushy beds. Further on, the blue glimmer of the pool and the solid lines of pale loungers stretched out expectantly under the watchful hillside, and the bright-faced moon above.

'This paradise and every other paradise like it will be hiding all sorts of cracks and holes and heartache.'

As she stared up at him lazily spearing watermelon and letting it slide down his throat, she recalled another article she had read, about his early childhood and humble beginnings.

'You had it tough at one point in time, didn't you?'

He raised an eyebrow, continued to munch melon and she watched in a hazy trance now as his muscled forearms flexed with each movement of his fork, and the thick column of his throat constricted with each swallow. It was poetry in motion, dark and male and utterly magnetic.

'No tougher than any other kid growing up in an abusive, dysfunctional family. All things considered, I had it pretty easy.'

'I'm sure you could take care of yourself,' she said, a trifle dismissively. He might have had humble beginnings but he had it all laid out at his feet now. He had no idea how she'd had to struggle.

'Well, you see, that's where you're wrong, Jacquelyn. I couldn't. So that's how I ended up here.'

He sounded so different, so quiet. He glanced down at the plate where a few glistening pink cubes of melon remained, but then he put his fork down, stared at it for a moment.

'I ran away. I met my wife at the side of the road when she was still someone else's wife. I knew what she was doing was wrong but I was eighteen. I was in so much trouble, with the police, with the gangs, with my father. I knew if I stayed in Sydney I'd be dead within a year. And then along comes Maria. And she wanted to be my wife and so I married her, I "reinvented myself" and now here I am. And here you are.'

As he spoke she felt the ghosts of his past swirl around. She saw him look at her, really look at her. He wasn't looking at her like a boss, he was looking at her like a man.

'Here we are indeed,' she said, and she glanced around with a nervousness that she wasn't sure was real.

'So, you see, I've bought the T-shirt with the whole marriage crap. It doesn't really do it for me now that I've grown up. No offence,' he said.

'None taken. For the record, I may work at one end of the marriage production line, but I'm well aware of how it can end up.'

'Things didn't work out for you either, did they?'

She flushed. She hated bringing all that up again. Not here, not now.

'Things worked out,' she said, but she couldn't meet his eye.

'Still hurts, huh? You're not alone. Men can tend to have the upper hand in relationships. Things seem a bit less complicated for us.'

'That's just an excuse for dishonourable people to act in a dishonourable way,' she said, and there was the bitterness in her voice, still there because she really didn't buy the argument that men were different from women. There were people who were good and there were people who weren't. There *were* good men in the world, like her father. The trouble was, they all appeared to be taken...

'OK. I hear you. But relationships come in many forms. I'm not saying it's OK to lie, but if everyone is clear about the boundaries, who are you to judge?'

'Not everyone is as clear about the boundaries as you think they are,' she said.

Nikos looked at her with understanding painted in his eyes.

'That Tim guy,' he said, quietly. 'What did he do to you?'

She'd told no one apart from her mother the facts of that night, but somehow the whole story had made it around town before she'd even taken her ring off and flushed it down the toilet.

'It's no secret. We were going out for four years, engaged for two and he left me five weeks before we were due to get married.'

He nodded. He reached over and squeezed her hand, but she drew it back again quickly.

'I'm sorry, but people split up, all the time. It happens. Better that it happened before you got married than after.'

'I know that. And believe me, I thank my lucky stars every day now. But it was how he did it. We were out for dinner. He ordered fillet steak, medium rare—he even said that—and then he just excused himself to go to the bathroom and never came back.'

She'd sipped her gin and tonic, watching the light dance off the self-same engagement ring, and feeling so proud and pleased that she would soon have a golden band there beside it. And she'd sipped some more as she'd waited on Tim, and then some more until she'd finished her drink. And then she'd realised, he was away too long. Far too long.

The shame, the humiliation. How long she had sat there, calling for help. *'My fiancé is stuck in the toilet...something must have happened to him. Please call the police...he's been abducted...'*

All the silly nonsense she'd convinced herself was true until, gently but firmly, the police officer had told her he had driven away in his own car—and had shown it to her there on the CCTV.

'That's pretty tough. You mean you didn't actually split up—he just split? Was there someone else?'

Nikos poured a little more wine, the gentle

slosh of liquid in the glass a mesmeric accompaniment to his words.

'I think so. I heard he went abroad, met someone else, a woman with children of her own. He's only been back in the country a few months.'

She wasn't going to tell him about the email he'd finally sent a month later. Saying it was all her fault, that she wouldn't listen. She'd driven him away.

'Rubbish,' her mother had said.

'I'll kill him if I get my hands on him,' her father had said.

'And yet you're "pure as the driven snow". Wasn't that what he called you?'

So he'd heard that. She wondered what else he'd heard. She swallowed and looked away.

'I might not have had the same experiences as some other people.'

'Experiences?' he asked. 'What kind of experiences are we talking about?'

How could he lace a simple word with such meaning? The hairs on the back of her neck stood up, a shiver ran through her and she forced herself to stare at her wine glass. She was hardly going to tell him about her sexual experiences, or lack of.

'I don't really care for the things other people care for.'

He watched her as he poured her another glass of wine. His eyes sparkled wickedly in the candlelight. He was as intoxicating as the wine. One more lingering stare and she'd be drunk. She reached for the water.

'You've been a good girl your whole life long.'

And look where it's got me, she thought, but sipped her water, said nothing. Being good was the only way she knew how to be. She didn't ask for it to be this way; she simply couldn't imagine any other way.

Her teenaged years with Tim had been innocent. They'd had their fun, but she'd been told by her mum and Nonna what wearing white meant. It had been drummed into her, like her date of birth, her address, her vital statistics.

All she'd wanted was to wait until they were married. What was so wrong with that? Why couldn't Tim do the same?

'Have you ever stepped onto the dark side, Jacquelyn?'

She swallowed, looked at him hard.

'I've never been tempted,' she said.

He smiled then and all over his face was temptation. In every hard line of his jaw, every brooding inch of his eyes, in the devilish swirl of his tattoo, she could see now, clearly, the other side of Nikos Karellis. The profit-driven retail mogul was gone and in his place was the Sydney Hell's Angel, and there was nothing remotely gentlemanly about him.

No more polite tolerance, no more board-meeting manners, now she was picking up something else entirely. Now he was seeing her as a woman, and nothing else.

Her heart thundered in her ears. Her body was swirling, she felt drunk, out of control, exhilarated, afraid.

'Never been tempted?'

He pushed away his plate and sat back, one hand resting on the white linen cloth. She shook her head. Things were shifting, the ground moving from under her, the world reforming into another place entirely. She was suddenly conscious of her legs, bare, her arms resting on the chair, her spine erect, the bodice of her dress with its revealing view of cleavage.

She pushed herself back from the table and the silk jersey of the dress slid over her bare legs as she crossed them, leaving her thigh exposed. He looked right there, at her leg, and she knew he liked what he saw.

'Not even a little?' he said, his fingers drumming a slow tattoo on the white linen.

Prickles of awareness swept over her arms, her legs and right to the tips of her breasts.

She felt a tingling at the nape of her neck. Her body was waking up from a long sleep. And it felt good. It felt exciting.

Her fingers curled around the cushion of the seat as she leaned forward to pull the skirt of the dress back over her legs.

'Leave that,' he whispered. 'Let yourself be tempted.'

Her breath quickened. Her heart picked up a strong, thudding beat. She felt herself rooted to the spot, hot and heavy and utterly under his spell. She was in very dangerous territory.

He pushed his chair back too, turned himself round to face her. She was afraid now— but only of herself and the calm, cool exterior that was slipping and sliding and beginning to feel like a puddle of watery ice at her feet.

Kiss me, kiss me, she thought, willing him closer. Her eyes fixed on his lips, her breasts ached under her dress and her back now arched into a curve all by itself, inviting him to savour her and take her.

But he sat there, just watching, drumming his fingers, slowly, slowly.

'I'll make the first move,' he said, and he stood then and closed the two steps to stand beside her. His groin was level with her eyes and her mouth. It was huge and she longed to reach out and touch him.

She was shocked, shocked that these thoughts were in her mind. And it was as if he knew. He stood still as a rock, watching her, then suddenly she felt his hand on the crown of her head, and with a jerk her head was tugged back.

'I bet you've got dark little thoughts and wicked fantasies in that head of yours.'

Her face flamed but she didn't try to deny it.

'I think you want me to forget why you're really here and lift you up and turn you in my arms and let you feel what you are only imagining.

'You want to taste it—it's so close now, Jacquelyn. It's right here. But you're still too afraid to let go.'

Her head was tilted up, her hair caught in a bunch in his hand, her lips were open and his face glowered down at hers, dark and deadly.

'I'm not afraid,' was all she said, her voice hoarse and throaty.

Slowly he raised her to standing, tugging her hair with just the most exquisite mix of pleasure and pain. And she was so close to him now she felt as if she was breathing in the very essence of maleness, the root and power of masculinity, and she was getting drunk on it.

'You want to know what it's like to make love to me.'

She would die rather than admit it, but silence was her confessor.

'And for a reason I still can't quite put my finger on, I am just as curious to know what it's like to make love to you.'

'I'm trying to take that as a compliment,' she said, rolling her head sensuously as his grip loosened to a caress.

'You should. It's been a very long time since I felt anything like this. A very long time. Maybe never...'

He trailed a finger down her cheek. Her eyes fluttered closed, her lips parted. She felt the finger land on the cushion of her lower lip. She would not give in so easily. She would not grab him the way she wanted to.

Seconds ticked by. His finger followed the lines of her lips, lightly dusted the edges of her cheekbones, the arcs of her eyebrows and with every passing moment she yearned for his lips.

'You know if we do this, Jacquelyn...you know what that means.'

Her head had fallen back and his arms scooped against her back, holding her steady as her neck lengthened in a gentle stretch. His fingers slid up to rest on her collarbone. And then she was closer still and she knew she was past the point of no return, that she had to feel his lips now…

'What does it mean?' she breathed.

Instead of answering, he now followed where his fingers had trailed from the base of her neck, with tiny feverish little kisses, brands. Up her neck to the apex where her jaw began, the most tender spot, so weakening her that her knees buckled.

'It means nothing. Just an amazing night, one amazing night. And tomorrow we go back to where we were.'

She heard his words and she felt his kisses, at her cheekbones, and she knew if she only waited, if she had the patience, if the seconds could only stop stretching for hours, days, weeks, that his lips would finally land on hers, that she would feel his kiss and taste him and know him.

And it was as if every moment of her life had been building to this. As if every single moment she'd ever spent as a girl, learning about her femininity, the way she walked and talked and held herself, the way she put on lipstick and painted her toenails, every moment was building into this, the essence of who she was as a woman.

Kiss me, she gasped, maybe aloud this time…

Her eyes were still closed but she knew he

was hovering over her face. She knew he was staring at her, at her opened lips. She felt her body throb with longing, she felt her nipples harden and ache for his hands. She arched her back and pressed closer to him, sinking into his maleness.

'I will kiss you. I'll kiss every part of you. But first…open your eyes, Jacquelyn.'

The rough rasping burr of his voice demanded and received. Her eyes flew open and she stared into his face. His eyes sparkled, points of light in the darkness, the black night sky behind.

'You understand what I am saying? This means nothing beyond pleasure. I don't owe you anything and you don't owe me. Your company and my company are nothing to do with this.'

'I understand,' she breathed, impatient for the sensations to return. If he had given her a contract to sign in blood she would have done it.

She stared at him, and when he didn't move she twisted out of his grasp and put her hands on his face, framing his mouth. She registered the surprise in his eyes, and heard the burst of black laughter that spilled from his throat.

'You are impatient, aren't you?'

But as she opened her mouth to speak he

grabbed her wrists and tugged them down to her sides. Her back arched and her breasts protruded and he growled and then finally, finally he placed his hot harsh kiss on her mouth. And his lips were hard and soft and wet and warm and she began to drown in each moment as the tug to have more and more began to tear at her. Then his tongue teased her lips apart, and now they duelled, and she gasped as another sharp tug built at her core. One of his hands now held her wrists, the other he trailed to her jaw, holding her steady.

'So we're clear—you'll not set this pace. That's not how things roll.'

She had never done anything more than kiss or caress a man. And she knew that none of the kisses or caresses had ever felt like this. Being close to him, the anticipation, each single moment was like a lifetime love affair in itself. The pleasure and pain of waiting, the exquisite heat that was building and building. She was emboldened. She was sexually confident in a way she'd never been before, she'd never known this language, these words and phrases, and she was desperate to start to converse.

'You don't really believe that,' she said, finding her voice. 'We both know who's really in control here.'

'You're deluded, Jacquelyn. You're mine. And I will do anything I want with you.'

'Anything?' she laughed.

She could barely keep the shivering desire from her voice. In the fleeting seconds she saw that she was in a new world. She'd never given away control of her body before, never fully relaxed.

Sex had once seemed part of a wonderful world that she would one day be given a map to arrive at. Then, it became this giant immovable structure that dominated everything, everywhere she looked, everyone was part of it and she was locked out.

She was tired of being the one on the outside. She wanted to know. She wanted to know so badly and she wanted to know now, tonight, with Nikos.

She didn't want to think about tomorrow, there was only now.

'I think you'd succumb to pretty much anything I asked.'

But still he did nothing other than glaze her with his eyes. Her spine felt bent as a bow, strung out, and his body was going to be the instrument that she played. She was almost reverberating with the tension of holding back. She longed to sing and throb and climb the heights with him. But she wasn't going to break and beg.

'You think very highly of yourself, don't you?' she asked, her voice tremulous and she knew he heard it too, because he smiled even more devilishly.

'When it comes to lovemaking? I think we both know the answer to that. You wouldn't be here if you didn't think the same.'

'Well, what are you waiting for?' she said.

'Good question.'

Then he bent his head low, to the exposed column of her neck. And she could see the crown of his head, the thick, dark crop of his hair. He released her wrist and she sank her fingers into his hair, holding him to her neck, her décolletage, her breasts. He growled as he nuzzled first one nipple, then the other. She heard a song in her own throat, a call from her heart.

Hungry, thirsty, greedy for every last bit of this man, she ran her hands over his head and down to his shoulders. She filled her palms with his muscle and drank deeply of the very air around him, the hot, humid night, the sky now bands of orange and mauve and the sun a tiny ball of gold sinking out of sight.

And like an addict craving more and more, she could not seem to get enough of his tongue, his lips, the pleasure he brought. She marvelled at the solid mass of muscle across his shoulders, ached to touch the skin beneath and slid her fingers to the buttons to begin her greedy exploration.

'Let's get comfortable,' he said, standing and scooping her up in his arms in one smooth movement.

Her laptop slid from the seat, from the corner of her eye she saw it land and fold, and as it hit the ground her heart sank with a moment of dread, as she remembered why she was really here and thought of what was still to come—the unfinished presentation, the half-baked plan...

But it was only a moment, a fleeting grey cloud of worry in this dazzling sky, and was gone, because she was up in his arms, her vision now his solid chest and the retreating terrace with all the ornaments of their brewing passion, the whisky bottle, the dining table, the half-drunk glasses of wine, the coffee pot, untouched, the candles flickering in the late evening breeze, to the billowing curtains of the daybed...

And then down she was placed. Soft mattress, cream curtains all around, tiny lights within the canopy like some fairy-tale chamber and there, proud and male and staring down at her like the warrior returned, Nikos.

She sat up on her elbows as he leaned over

her and their lips found each other in a new familiarity. His tongue claimed hers, hot breath
and wet mouths, his scent, his skin, his utterly
irresistible Nikos-ness had her scrabbling up,
holding him while he pulled off his shirt.

And then she saw what she had needed to
see, and he was magnificent and marvellous
and she felt as if she was reeling at the sight.
His shoulders, broad and golden, and biceps,
inked and hard, and his chest, wide and dark,
and his nipples, small and flat and beaded,
and it was there her tongue went, as her hands
touched and stroked and grabbed and she filled
all of her senses with this man.

What on earth had she been imagining? Not
this! This was so much more, so wonderful.
The more male he was, the more she felt her
own femininity, the more emboldened she was.
So this was making love. She was awake and
alive for the first time in her life.

She felt his arms slide under her shoulders;
her legs wrapped around his waist as if they
had a hundred times before.

'Take your dress off,' he said in a growl.

His words splashed water on her fever, and
she slid back from the discovery of his body to
look up into his face. For a moment he looked
distant, his eyes dark and impassioned, as if

the fire that burned was darker now, and the light behind his eyes was almost out.

For one horrible second a laser point of fear burned in her heart. She was on fire with lust, dishevelled, her dress around her waist, her breasts soaked with his mouth, her nipples taut, but the sweetness had gone, the sense that something uniquely special was building between them. Now she could be anyone lying here in this chamber.

She could still stop this now. She could roll over, fix her clothes, run back to the terrace, collect her laptop and turn back into the person she really was. She had her life, her business, her family name, her little courtyard and her shop. She was never going to be this woman again. She had opened the door but she didn't need to run through it.

But then he moved. Back. He stepped back as if he sensed what she was thinking. He pulled out of the fiery circle that had been burning around them and she felt the chill of that. Was he having second thoughts? His eyes were trained on her but it was concern she saw there; she saw it and she scorned it. She didn't want his concern, or anybody else's.

She was sick of being Jacquelyn Jones. She was sick of being the devoted daughter whose only goal in life was to replicate the goals of all the people who came before her. She was sick of waiting for a fantasy that hadn't come true. This was her fantasy now—here in Greece, in the villa of one of Europe's best lovers, and she would never be here again...

In a moment she was up on her knees. She threw her arms around his neck and she found his mouth and she kissed him with everything she had.

He paused, he stilled, and then the fire erupted in seconds, the roar of his voice and the cry from her throat as he, one-handed, laid her down, and unfastened his belt and flies and she scrambled out of her dress.

Her eyes and hands started to grab for him, the huge silken-tipped beautiful manly thrust of him, but he grabbed her wrists and shook his head.

'Ladies always come first,' he said, and then he dropped to his knees, and eased hers apart and placed his head where she longed to see it, and instead of rejecting, because she knew in her heart that there would never be another touch like his, she lay back and let him call the song from her heart with every lap of his tongue.

The bloom of her orgasm built from every pore of her body to her core, one huge wave of pleasure, and she screamed his name as pulse after pulse rocked her.

And as she sank back he was there, naked, sheathing himself masterfully, his eyes boring into her face, his own desire as boldly painted as the inked designs on his chest. His arm was now under her back, her chest lifted, her neck stretched and her head falling back, and then she was down again and he was sliding his shaft inside her body, and as it closed around him, inch by inch, the flash of pain was buried by the last moments of her beautiful, heart-melting orgasm.

But her eyes opened into his face, watching, and she killed his questioning look with a smile and a kiss and a silent prayer of thanks for making her first time better than her wildest dreams.

She squeezed her thighs and urged him on, and he pushed himself inside her, his body sliding over hers, the weight and warmth, the strength and power rubbing against her soft tender flesh and nothing in the world had ever felt as good as this. She relished it like the best food and wine, the best sunset, the softest silk. Nothing was as good now, nothing would ever be as good again.

Her lips kissed and tasted, her hands roamed everywhere—his hair, his muscled back; she grabbed for the sheets of the daybed, then back to him again, as he thrust and built it up all over again.

Then a cry came from his throat, the start of a noise that built—he pushed himself back from her and, bereft of his body, she reached forward and licked at his nipple, flat and hard—and he opened his eyes and smiled, sweetly—he smiled and she licked again and then he started to thrust hard and fast and he was going to orgasm, she could feel the moment swirl and swell between them.

It was all she needed to join him. Like two animals writhing, loving under the light of the stars, lost in passion.

And then it was over. He rolled onto his back, threw his arm above his head. She rolled with him, as if tugged by a magnet, and watched as he blew out a long sigh. He shook his head, first with a kind of incredulity and then as if to settle everything back down to normal.

She lay back beside him, gazing up at the tented roof of the daybed, the tiny lights twinkling down, witnessing their heartbeats slowing, and the cool realisation of each second ticking by, knowing that what was once hidden was now known.

'Are you OK?' he asked, but without moving.

She waited a moment before replying as the images flashed through her mind.

'Perfectly well, thanks,' she said.

He leaned up on one elbow, stared at her.

'For a moment I thought you were a virgin.'

'No. I'm not a virgin,' she said. *Not any more.*

Because technically it was true, and he didn't need to know her truth—not right now. She'd tell him later, because all she wanted to feel now was the relief, the joy of being part of a world that she'd never been able to visit before. She wasn't a little girl any more, she was a woman. A healthy, happy, normal and free woman.

What a truly beautiful experience. What an amazing man…

'My mistake,' he said.

His eyes were soft, his mouth in a smile, his face mere inches away; that special moment bloomed again, that calling to her that this was all OK, that she hadn't been crazy to do this, that she was safe.

Yes, that she was safe…

'Shall we see if we can feel any better than "perfectly well"? Based on first impressions, I think we might just manage it.'

He was leaning even closer and now mingled in with the man was the scent of them and, like a switch, on it went—her lust and longing. Her body turned towards him, complicit and willing, and she was welcomed back into his arms with a smile that turned into a kiss, that turned into an embrace and, with a laugh in her throat that startled her, she was swept up in his arms, and on through the night, to the house.

And with every step she felt a tremor of anxiety, and with every breath she batted it away. This was one night. One night. And all her tomorrows were ahead of her. Nothing was going to change how they passed. Nothing she could do now was going to change a single thing, other than her memories.

CHAPTER SEVEN

GHOSTS. HE HAD never believed in them. It didn't make sense that the dead were still among the living. When your time was up, that was it. Life was bearable if he thought of it that way. But being back here in Greece, he had suddenly started to see them.

Not spectres as such, but the ghosts of his past—images and feelings that had been hanging around, just out of sight. In the corner of a room, the curl of a smile, the heat of day.

Memories—that was all they were, but there was nothing sweet about them. Nothing sweet about that feeling of fear that a hand, or worse, was about to come down on the back of your head, or that the path towards the light had suddenly turned rocky and unsafe, that the love you had once had turned sick—a shiny red apple, bored through and turned rotten by the ravenous worm of addiction and greed.

That was the way it had become with Maria.

Now that he knew that love was simply lust, a rush of hormones, temporary blindness, like staring into the sun for too long. His crazy re-action to Maria had been no more than two lost souls finding one another, the bigger the holes inside them, the bigger the fall. Think-ing she could fill the hole in him had been the biggest mistake of his life.

Nobody could fill that gaping wound except his House, his world. House was his wife and child, his family.

Nikos stood on the clifftop terrace and braced his hands on the screen that separated him from the deep, still Aegean Sea. How many times had he stood here, staring out across the blues of daybreak and dusk, bro-ken only by the scattering of islands and boats, slowly skating past?

He'd loved this place once. He hadn't re-alised just how much until he was back here, feeling peace settling slowly around him, en-joying those last few minutes before the world started to waken and decisions had to be made.

He should be sleeping now, he should have squeezed the last balm of rest before starting the day, because he was going to need to stand firm and not allow himself to be swayed by his incredibly strong attraction to Jacquelyn Jones.

His one rule, his North Star, for years had

been: will this make money? Will this make the board and my shareholders happy? If not, there was no space for it. No dead weights, no millstones, nothing but relentless progress forward. It was his mark as a leader—shedding the brands and products that didn't fit, even if they were profitable in the short term, for the sake of House.

Ariana Bridal was a company of the past, not the future. He could give Jacquelyn business advice, but he couldn't take her on. Not now. Especially not now.

He'd known this yesterday, he'd known it before he'd even agreed to this stupid idea and he cursed his own weakness in indulging his sexual side at the expense of cold-blooded business.

But it wasn't just that, was it? There was something sick inside him. Something that he kept buried with every eighteen-hour working day, and every scholarship he funded, and every woman he took to his bed. He buried the evil that was there—smothered it—but last night it had surfaced.

He glanced over to the smooth blue pool, its quiet surface untouched and flat. Beyond it, half-obscured by the thick hedge, sat the hot tub. He didn't shudder now when he thought of it. He could walk past it and he didn't see his father sitting back in it, his shaved head, his tough muscular shoulders, the incongruous tattoos of a rose on one bicep and a mermaid on the other, on arms that had literally choked the life from people who got in his way...

The hot tub had been drained but its empty blue shell still sat, right beside the daybed. Its tented roof poked now above the hedge, innocently concealing the scene of their crazy lovemaking.

He'd almost lost control. He'd been all the way to hell and back with every sip of whisky—the memories of his father and finding him with Maria, right there, in that tub. His taunts, her screaming, begging...

He hung his head in shame.

His hatred and his guilt had sprung back last night like a black geyser, forced through the earth. It was as if none of the five years since had made one blind bit of difference. The plaster was ripped back off and nothing could stop the pain but a beautiful blonde with soft curves and a sweet smile.

And it *had* stopped it for those brief, sweet hours. The pain had gone, the memories faded away in that woman's arms and the world had paused while he found solace. It was as if he were making love again for the first time, it was new and fresh and it felt—right? It felt as if he was with someone pure; there was no other way of putting it.

But she wasn't here for him. She was here to save her business. Everyone had their reasons and those were hers. He didn't despise her for it, but he wasn't going to hang on to the fantasy he'd built up that she was some kind of Goody-Two-Shoes and he was her knight in shining armour. She was as happy as he was to share a warm bed, but the bottom line was that she was here for her business, not for anything else.

He turned to look through the glass, a glimpse of the bed through the split in the curtains. The bed where she lay, naked, tangled in a sheet, where even the thought of her made him once again react. Any other time than this he'd be happy to slide into that warm bed. But he'd been round the block too many times. Business first. Then pleasure.

He gripped the railing and shook his head.

He had to put a stop to this. He had to gather the papers and deliver them to Mark.

At a sound behind him, he turned to look back over his shoulder. The curtains wafted in the breeze, lifting to show the bed, now empty, the imprint of their bodies clear on the sheets. He stepped into the room, sensing her, following the invisible trail through the air. A door closed further inside. The sound of the shower…

The party was over. They'd made the deal, had their fun, and now they had to get on with it.

He made his way to the other end of the house, showered and dressed and sent a maid to Jacquelyn with a message—breakfast would be served on her terrace, in the guest room. He would meet her in the boardroom at eight-thirty.

Half an hour to hear her pitch and then they'd fly back to London. It wouldn't be a pleasant flight but she was a big girl. She'd get over it.

Then on to New York where he'd take the papers to Mark himself. They'd have to sit down together, go through everything, find the trail and deal with it.

What would happen next would happen. It was out of his control. The last thing he wanted to do was involve the police but if it came to it—well, if it came to it, all hell would have been already unleashed.

And much as it pained him to leave this little corner of Greece, there was nothing here for him now. His mother would never see it again, and there was no one left who even remembered her. He'd sell this house and everything in it and he would close, hopefully once and for all, this chapter in his life.

Jacquelyn's head pounded as if she had a bass drum for a brain. Her stomach flipped butterflies up into her chest and her body ached in a thousand different places.

She dried her hair and put on make-up and looked at the reflection in the mirror. Nothing to see. No cracks showing. Her hair was sleek, her skin was smooth, her eye sockets were camouflaged and she had smudged highlighter where shadows lurked. She looked... OK.

She looked OK, but no matter how long she'd stood in the shower she still couldn't wash away the dirty sense of guilt, the feeling that she had let herself down, and that feeling had clung to every sweep of her mascara wand, every smoothing brush of her hair. No matter how many tricks she played, the face that stared back at her was wretched and desperate and...sad.

So she had waited, her whole life long she had been the one who was saving herself for her wedding day. She put so much store on love and marriage, and sex was the expression of a lifetime promise to the man she would spend her whole life with.

She could laugh out loud but it really wasn't funny. The one time she'd decided to let herself go was the one time she should have been keeping it all together.

The saving grace was that unlike the last time she'd made such a monumental fool of herself, no one was here to witness her stupidity.

No one who knew her would ever think she'd throw her whole existence up in the air, especially when it involved jumping into bed with a man she'd only just met. And she clearly hadn't made that great an impression. Even though she had felt so close to him, so sure that he was feeling what she was feeling, that this passion was surely unique, that their love-making couldn't possibly end after one night—other thoughts entirely must have been running through his mind. So much so that he'd left in the middle of the night, leaving her to awaken cold and alone in an empty bed.

She'd slid her hands across the sheets to feel for warmth but there was none; he must have been gone for ages. She'd sat up, looked around in the darkness at the unfamiliar shapes of his room. She tried to remember what had happened. Should she try to find him? Should she be worried? In the end she had buried herself in the bed and curled into a ball, her mind whirling with the awful realisation that she'd been abandoned, not held lovingly, not caressed or kissed.

It's fine, it's fine, she told herself in between forcing slow, deep breaths. *It's just the shock. You're overreacting. It's because of what happened with Tim and this isn't the same at all. This is all OK. It was just sex. He's just a man.*

Why was she so unlucky?

Why couldn't she choose someone who would really care for her? Her mother had found her father. Other people found happy, faithful partners. Why not her? What was she doing wrong?

Well, there was nothing else for it now. All that she could do was make the best of it. She had to pick herself up all over again and get on with it.

You're better than this. You have to do what you came here to do and go down to this meeting, head held high.

She had better stand there in front of him and sell this business and forget those hours writhing naked in bed with him, screaming his name and feeling him lose himself in her, over and over again. She couldn't possibly come all this way and go home with nothing—nothing other than the memory of one night of passion.

But still she sat, staring, numb. Behind her

the bed she should have slept in, smooth and intact, a monument to her guilt. She checked her watch. Eight-fifteen. Any minute now she was going to get up from this stool and slip into yesterday's crushed sundress. She was going to walk through this sprawling villa, not thinking all her excited, girlish thoughts, and become the stony-faced businesswoman she had to be.

She wasn't going to use facts and figures and numbers and charts. That wasn't her best language and right now she didn't have the head for it at all. She was going to speak from the heart. She would tell him the real story of Ariana Bridal and how her grandmother had built it from nothing, sewing her own dreams with the dreams of the women whose wedding gowns she'd stitched. She was going to tell him of the tiny shop and how it smelled of flowers and how, as a child, she'd longed to touch the white and creamy silks, and had loved to see the faces of the women who'd tried on dresses, expectant, puzzled and then finally the beaming smiles as each of them had looked like the bride they would be.

She wasn't going to tell him that she had wished with all her heart that she would be one of those brides one day, dressed in white, making her *nonna* proud.

No, what she would tell him was that the tiny shop had become two then three, then more, each of them uniquely, expertly caring for each bride. How could that tiny empire wither and die now when it had so much of what women really wanted? That personal touch...women who understood other women?

That little shop held her dreams safe inside, like an egg in a nest: her dreams, her mother's health, her father's income—everything she held dear was caught up in Ariana Bridal.

How clearly she could still see her grandmother's tiny hands, one buried in silk, the other busily hand-stitching pearls.

A tear formed in her eye. She tipped her head back, desperately holding it in place. She would not cry again. *Please not now...*

She stood up tall, she breathed, and just as she heard the footsteps of the maid she smiled a tiny smile and turned, ready.

On they walked to the boardroom. With every step along the hallway, her heels echoed in the marbled void but her thundering, anxious heartbeat all but smothered her sense of hearing.

She saw a door ahead, and she knew this was it. The maid paused, Jacquelyn rounded the corner of the room and he looked up at her, their eyes meeting in a flash of recognition and acknowledgement. And—damn it to hell—shame.

He waited until the maid closed the door behind them.

'Good morning, Jacquelyn. I hope you found everything you needed this morning.'

'Yes, thanks,' she repeated, automatically.

'Great, well, let's do this. I'm sure you are as desperate to get back to England as I am to get across the Atlantic. I've got meetings set up for the rest of the day so, shall we?'

Complete denial that they had spent the night making love? She had expected a businesslike approach but this was callous even beyond that.

'I've had your laptop hooked up over there.'

He bowed his head to his own machine, cast a hand to the end of the long shiny table where a screen blinked down from the wall.

She looked back to see his dark head bent, his brow furrowed, his hands flying over the keyboard, sending emails as she stood there. He didn't even have the grace to pay her any attention.

'I'm not going to use technology,' she said.

He looked up, his brow furrowed even more. Standing there, she felt like a schoolgirl with unfinished homework.

'You're not? I thought you were working on something yesterday.'

'That was yesterday,' she said. She heard the wobble in her voice but it wasn't grief. It was anger. Pure, cold anger.

'Look, before you begin… Jacquelyn,' he said, pushing back from the desk and sitting up straight in his chair. 'What happened last night was just sex. It has nothing to do with this. I hope I made it clear that the two things are totally unconnected.'

She hadn't expected him to be so *cold*, so brutal. It was as if he were putting oceans of distance between them before she had even begun. He wasn't even giving her a chance. Dragging her here and then all that they had done, and now he was rejecting not only her body but her business too…?

'You said it didn't count,' she heard her voice say. 'You didn't say it would disadvantage me.'

'I didn't exactly say that.'

'You didn't have to. It's written all over your face.'

'Fair enough,' he conceded, after a long pause. A pause in which she felt as if her whole world were contaminated. But damn him, damn his dark mood and his thin-lipped smile, damn his broad shoulders and wash-board-flat abs. Damn his hands that had held her and caressed her and his whole wretched body that had pounded into hers, pounding as her heart was now pounding in her own ears.

'Fair enough,' he said again, but it was without enthusiasm. It was a concession to her boldness, a momentary victory.

'So, can you at least tell me if I'm wasting my time?' she asked. 'I'd rather know now. I don't really want to be here any more than you do. I am very well aware that you've filed what happened last night under "No Further Action".'

He smiled now, to himself, clearly amused at her imagining that anything else was ever likely to have happened.

'Go on,' she said. 'Deny it.'

Her voice was shrill with anger. She couldn't quite believe what was happening, but it seemed to be out of her hands now. Words were pouring out of her mouth.

'Who are you angry with, Jacquelyn? Me, for making the first move, or yourself for thinking I'd fall into line.'

'I'm not angry with myself. I'm not the one with double standards.'

'Maybe not. But you wouldn't be the first woman to think that sleeping with me would get you preferential treatment. It's the oldest trick in the book.'

'How dare you?' she said, white rage now slipping over her. 'You have no idea who I am or what I stand for. But it's quite obvious what goes on inside your head.'

She turned around, as if she could grab her coat and make for the nearest exit and hail a black cab on the street, but all she saw was a blinking blank screen and his reflection outlined in it. She kept her face turned there, feeling the tears welling up and her chin wobbling and that dreadful thickening warning of grief in her throat.

Months she had been like this. Months recovering from that rat Tim, and now here she was back again. A gibbering, soft-hearted idiot who couldn't even stand up for herself.

Every single fibre in her body thrummed with fury at herself. She would not turn round and show him. Not one single sign of weakness. Not one.

But the energy in the room shifted and she watched as, like a typhoon cloud crossing the plain, the image in the screen moved and in seconds he was standing there behind her.

She looked down at her fingers curled white around the back of the chair. She concentrated all her strength into that single spot, tried to repel him with the sheer force of her will, just as she had opened herself up to him last night—welcomed his kisses, his touch, his body. Welcomed them and lost herself in them.

How on earth could she have been so completely naive?

'Look,' he said, his voice low and calm. 'I'm sorry. That came out all wrong. I just don't want you to get your hopes up. I've had a look through your website and it's not going to work for House. That's it. I don't mind giving you a hand, you know. A mentoring partner or something like that. I can advise on various things that you might find useful. But…'

'My family poured everything into this business. My grandmother's fingers were curled with arthritis by the age of fifty but she stitched and made beautiful clothes for the women of our town, and she would be ashamed to see me standing here like this.'

'The last thing I want is for you to feel ashamed. I'm just trying to keep it business-like from now on.'

Jacquelyn turned around. She swallowed the bitter pill of self-pity and guilt and lifted her head to face him. Tears were welling in her eyes and her throat was burning but she was damned if she was going to take his crumbs. No matter what happened to Ariana now, she would never stand there begging from a man like him.

'I don't need to say any more to you. I just need you to arrange my transport home.'

Beyond his head the day was shimmering into another dreamy Grecian morning. There wasn't a cloud in the sky, not a ripple on the sea, nothing other than heat and light and promise. And somehow that made her feel even worse.

She had no business being here—she should be back home in Lower Linton, opening up the shop, checking the flowers in the hallway, making sure the staff were pristine and smiling welcomes to the clients, checking the work in progress, the fittings and deliveries, the goodness knew what. There was so much to be done. She had to get away, get back to work, immediately.

She went to brush past the solid wall standing in her way, but he didn't step back and she bounced back just as his hand reached out and grasped her arm.

'Look, I apologise.'

His voice was rough, his grip was strong but she jerked her arm away, hating the heat of his hands and the closeness of his body and the wide wall of his shoulders that obscured her view.

'That really isn't going to make any difference now,' she said. 'Your apology doesn't count for very much and I've got too much to do today so, as I said, can you organise my transport?'

And with that she walked out of the room. She didn't know which way she was going, only that she was heading away from him— nowhere was far enough away. She'd damn well keep walking all the way to England if she had to.

She turned around another corner and the tears were coming—she felt them burn and bubble up. Her eyes were glassy and sightless.

'Jacquelyn, wait!' he thundered.

But she wasn't going to wait for his storm. She was going home under her own steam.

She stumbled along the corridors, the forest of doors, wrong turnings, like being lost in a maze of her own anger and shame.

Thank God no one could see her. Thank God her mother and father were safe in Spain. What on earth was she going to tell them about this? She had to get out of here, away, home.

She found the room. She found her bag, keys, phone, passport, purse.

The sea was to her left, the road to her right. She put her head up and followed the shining marble hallways to the front of the house. No one tried to stop her. And just as well for them that they didn't.

There were the two huge wooden doors she'd come in through. She pulled and pulled at one of them until it finally groaned open.

Heat and light hit her first. A car parked in the turning circle, the plants deep and exotic, a driveway, olive groves on either side, a dusty road, and that was where she walked now, her heels stupid and her toes crushed and her mind whirring with desperate scenarios of how she was going to get home...

And then suddenly along the driveway, a car appeared, driving straight past her. She jumped into the side of the road. The window was lowered and a face with dark glasses peered at her. Then it stopped, reversed back, the door opened. A man got out, a bodyguard? Another one got out the other side.

Instinctively she stopped. She could see her reflection in the window. She looked back at the house and then round to the two men. They didn't move.

This didn't feel right. This didn't feel right at all.

CHAPTER EIGHT

NIKOS STOOD, UNBELIEVING. As unable to move as the pillars propping up the roof of the million-dollar home beside him, watching this hideous scene unfold.

Even from here he could make out the scar on the man's face, the glowering brows, the busted left arm and the hunched shoulders.

His father's best friend, Bruno. Fifteen years older but still as menacing and standing right there in his driveway, still oozing venom, the menacing killing machine that terrorised even the dirtiest, darkest criminals in Sydney.

'Jacquelyn, come back here,' he heard himself bark out.

He shifted his gaze from Bruno and stared at her, willing her back with the force of his gaze. She swung her head slowly round to look at him, and he saw fear sweep over her face, but she didn't move.

'Now,' he growled.

And he could see her waver, he could see her falter in her path. She couldn't possibly go forward. No one could walk into that and not feel the danger. And he wouldn't let her face that, in a million years.

His feet started to move, his arms tensed and his hands bunched into fists, worthless he knew against whatever was in the pockets of the jackets they wore. These men didn't fight with fists, they had bars, and knives and guns and anything else that got their message across. He'd seen them. He'd felt them. He'd screamed silently in nightmares remembering.

Time seemed to have stopped. He was aware of his heart, his gut, the swirls of dust in the road. Jacquelyn swung her head again, her golden hair catching every sunbeam, but her eyes were filled with dark, cold fear. Her arms wrapped around her body and she turned to him with a questioning, terrified look on her face.

And it was as if he saw his mother's face, and remembered her fear and his fear, and he would not let this happen again.

He was at her side, reaching for her, tugging her to him, spinning her round behind him.

'Get off my land, Bruno!' he roared. 'Get out of here now and tell whoever sent you that there's nothing here for him.'

'You know who sent me,' said Bruno. 'He wants what he's due.'

He didn't want any of this aired. He didn't want anyone else touched by this evil.

'Get back in the house,' he hissed to her. 'Please don't argue.'

But she didn't move. She had melted against him. He felt the weight of his body shield her, and she let him be that shield, and he was more grateful for that than anything. The closeness was there, back around them, this strange physical intimacy that made him want to roar and beat his chest and kill anything that tried to harm the soft, trusting body that he held now under his arm.

Every second that passed made him swell with anger that she was exposed to this. That this sewer had once more flooded the brilliant Grecian world, that somehow his past was here, now, facing him down.

'He should be rotting in jail. That's what he's due.'

'That's never going to happen, Nikos. We both know that.'

'One day.'

Bruno shook his head.

'You're making a mistake, Nikos,' he said as he tracked his steps back to the car and got in. 'He'll come and find you. And he won't be as nice as me.'

The doors closed. The engine started, and then slowly the car began to reverse down the driveway, as dust clouds spilled up from the ground and birds circled high overhead.

Nikos and Jacquelyn stood there until it swung round and the blinking red brake lights disappeared. Neither of them spoke. Her body was still pressed close and his arm held her in place, safe. His heart thundered, and then slowed. The morning settled, and sparkled and righted itself again, as if nothing had ever happened.

At the same moment they pulled apart.

'I'm sorry you had to witness that.'

'They had guns, didn't they?'

'Let's talk about this inside.'

He looked around, half expecting to see them coming back, but everything was quiet, just as it should be. Hot, bright and beautiful.

He shook his head, hating every single thing that was happening. Hating that Bruno had polluted his world. Hating his father. But mostly hating his own fear. He should have faced up to him before now. He should have met him, somewhere, anywhere, sorted whatever needed to be done. But he was a coward when it came to his father. No matter how much he wanted to do it, he just couldn't take the steps he needed to take.

'My legs are like jelly,' she said, and he scooped her up into his arms, holding her even more tightly than he needed, expecting her to push him away, but she didn't move, didn't push back, didn't reject him in any way. And that made him even more furious with himself.

No matter that she was barely an acquaintance, a never-to-be-repeated one-night stand, an out-of-her-depth businesswoman—she was his guest, on his land, at his invitation, and she should never, ever have been exposed to this.

Two more strides to the front doors. He kicked them open, walked in and kicked them closed again. She was still buried against his chest.

He stared around wondering where to go, what to do, how to make this better. Tea. She was English and the English had tea to solve everything.

The kitchen was empty of staff, thank God; they had all gone to Agios Stephanos, the little church on the hillside, to celebrate the saint's day. Jacquelyn slipped out of his arms and into a chair, burying her hands in her hair, and he felt the loss of setting her down as if he'd removed a sheepskin coat in the harshest winter.

'Who were they?' she said, looking up at

him, and the look on her face crushed him, squeezed his hard, iron heart.

The only thing that would make this better was honesty.

'They were—they are—criminals.'

Jacquelyn didn't look away from his hard, determined gaze, the one he was using to hold himself in check, to tell her that he wasn't lying.

'Gangsters. From Sydney.'

'They're why you ran away,' she said, as if to herself. 'You were mixed up with people like that and you ran away.'

'Something like that,' he conceded.

'I think I deserve a better answer than that,' she said, her voice slicing right through his self-pity.

He swallowed hard. What part of his past could he share with someone like her? His mother's bruises? Her brain haemorrhage? Maria's last few months on this earth, her drinking and drug-taking, siphoning money from every asset she could get her hands on to pay for her habits. She had sold everything she could, all that was left was herself. He could still hear her pleading cries. He could still feel his disgust, his rejection, his father's laughter. The sight of her car. There had been no hope.

'You might not have the stomach for it.'

'Give me some credit, Nikos. I've just come face to face with armed men. I think I can listen to the backstory.'

He turned and looked at her sitting there, one elbow on the table, spine straight and face composed. The woman he'd held in his arms, the woman who had travelled hundreds of miles to save her business. The woman he'd dismissed without so much as a kind word and who'd kept her cool in front of those low-life scum.

But confessing was tantamount to informing. It was drilled in him so deeply, even if he wanted to say it, he didn't think he had the words.

'He was,' he began slowly, trying them out, '...is, my father's lieutenant.'

A frown crossed her brow, like a prompt for him to continue.

'And my father is one of the most notorious gang leaders—drugs, counterfeit money, that sort of thing. He was selling drugs to Maria the night she died.'

There. He'd said it. And she didn't even flinch.

'I see. So "he wants what he's due" means payment for the drugs?'

'He's also saying that he gave her money to invest.'

'Do you mean money laundering?' she asked, her eyes widening.

He nodded.

'I think so. The Inland Revenue also want what they're due—the whole thing is a mess and we, my accountant and I, can only find bits of the trail. I want to find the clues before they do—it'll look a hell of a lot better. The last thing I want to be accused of is money laundering.'

'No, it's not a good look,' she said, but without any trace of humour.

'None of this is a good look. The whole thing is a mess until I can clear my dad completely out of my life. I'm going to risk this kind of thing happening again if I don't. And I can't have gangsters turning up in Agios Stephanos. I can't bring this sort of trouble here.'

'Well, short of going to the police I don't see what else you can do.'

He walked to the window, a wall of glass that offered the panorama of rocky cliffs and wide, deep blue sea. There was no place on earth like it.

'I love this place so much, but even when I'm not here it's not safe. There was a burglary six months back. I'm sure it was them.'

'You have to go to the police,' she said.

He didn't even answer that. People didn't understand. The police wouldn't solve anything; they'd only create more problems. Gangs had reach far beyond the law, more terrifying ways than a stretch in jail.

'Well, what else can you do? Apart from sell it?'

Sell the house he'd designed himself, hoping he could one day bring his mum back to it, so she could sit on the terrace and stare at the Aegean, hear the cicadas and taste the olives. That was never going to happen now anyway. One more infection and her body would shut down completely.

'I built this place for myself, but it deserves a family,' he said, looking around, suddenly seeing the answer in rooms full of children running, playing, laughing. 'I'd like to give the local people real work to do, instead of looking after a museum.'

He put the steaming cup in front of her. She nodded at it, muttered a thank you.

'I can see it too,' she said, gazing around, as if the ghosts of the future appeared for her too. She smiled and took a sip of the tea, making a slight face as she put it down.

'The tea OK?'

She smiled up at him then.

'It's hot and tastes vaguely of tea.'

'Jacquelyn, I'm sorry.'

'Oh, don't worry. It's perfectly palatable.'

'I'm not talking about the tea.'

'Oh. Well,' she said, flicking her eyes at him. 'I don't hold you responsible. You didn't look any more pleased to see them than I did.'

'For everything. For dragging you here, for getting drunk last night. For taking advantage—'

'I'll stop you right there. You didn't take advantage of me. I didn't do anything I didn't want to do. But your accusation was unforgivable.'

She spoke quietly, shaking her head, and that simple fact twisted his gut even more.

'You're right,' he said, holding up his hands. 'I was angry with the world, with myself—and I took it out on you. You know I had a great night. An amazing night.'

She looked up then, just a flash of those sky-blue eyes. The last time he'd seen that look he'd thought her coy, but not now—this time, there was no smile on her lips, no playful dip of her eyelashes.

He waited for her to speak, to say the words he realised now he wanted to hear back—that she'd loved it too, that it was special for her, that it wasn't just a little bit of action to pave the way for a sweeter deal.

'I made my own bed, so to speak, and now I've got to lie in it.'

'That's an interesting choice of image, if you don't mind me saying.'

He looked again hoping for even a hint of a smile, but there was nothing other than the implacable composure he'd been presented with when he'd first met her. It was the glassy surface of a pond, the swan gliding, but there had to be something going on under there. It just wasn't natural to be so composed. He'd liked it better when she'd let go, in the two times he'd seen her do it…last night in the bedroom, and this morning in the boardroom.

He wasn't the type to pussyfoot around a subject, and this was bothering him now. They had amazing chemistry. The best. It wasn't the sexual World Championships but she was sweet and innocent and incredibly sexy—how many women had he ever met who made him feel the way he'd felt last night?

It was as if the dirt and grime and muck of the past fifteen years had been rinsed off. As if he'd discovered making love all over again. And he assumed she'd felt exactly the same— dammit, at times she'd made him think she'd never made love before, her reactions were so raw, so visceral.

'Are you regretting the fact that we had sex?'

'Bitterly,' she said, as if she had said, *Pass me the milk.*

'OK,' he said, absorbing that like a slap.

She stood up. She walked to the cupboards, opening doors and looking inside, and without any invitation began to make herself another cup of tea.

She looked at home. She looked very much at home, and it startled him out of his dark daydreams. He'd never let any woman have the run of his house since Maria.

'Would you like another tea?' she asked, turning to stare over her shoulder. She was so beautiful, so feminine, so *right*?

The word formed in his mind and something twisted inside him, something uncomfortable.

'No, you go on right ahead yourself though. *Mi casa es su casa*, and all that.'

In the act of pouring the water into the cup, she stopped. Cool, calm sky-blue eyes blinked at him.

'Let's not get carried away. You practically threw me out earlier, remember?'

'Now, hang on, Jacquelyn. I didn't throw you out. I was being honest with you. I might have been a bit brusque but there wasn't any point in having you go through all the pain of a full-blown pitch for me to turn round and say no. My mind was already made up.'

She put the kettle down with a thump and turned right round to face him.

'What point, exactly, in this fantasy trip did you make your mind up? Before or after we had sex?'

She might be feminine but she was fierce! She was indomitable. She was every bit the boardroom commander and she almost took his breath away. Nobody could hold a candle to her now, standing here like this.

'Answer me,' she said.

'OK. Since you're asking me a direct question, I'll give you a direct answer. I knew before we had sex that I wasn't going to offer you a business deal. I knew it before you got on the plane. I probably knew it before I agreed to the breakfast meeting.'

A flush of roses on her cheeks was all that he could see but he could feel her anger. He wanted to haul her into his arms and kiss her, and it was getting harder and harder to stand with his arms folded across his chest and a cup of tea in his hand.

'You took me all this way, knowing that you were wasting my time—just to have sex?'

'No. I took you all this way, presuming I might be wasting your time, because I made a commitment to my former brother-in-law, who coerced me into meeting with you because he felt sorry for you, and I had no intention of having sex with you at the start of this. None.

In fact, it's pretty much the only intention that I have reneged on in the past year.'

'I can't believe this,' she said, turning her back on him. 'You've made me feel like a complete idiot.'

He sighed. 'I wanted to help you. I liked you. I was incredibly attracted to you and last night—there was so much going on…in my life.'

'So it was just a case of right time, right place. She'll do.'

'That's not how it was.'

The roses on her cheeks had bloomed now and her eyes blazed blue. If he'd been aiming for a better understanding he'd completely failed. He could feel himself getting into dangerous waters and he cursed this stupid situation. He cursed his indebtedness to Maria, and the cord that linked him back to his father. He cursed the whole damn lot of them that had now caught this woman up in the mess of his life.

He cursed it because she was a breath of clean air, and now he felt as if even she had been polluted.

'Well, that's how it felt to me, so do you see how it makes me feel? Do you?'

She spoke with pain in her voice and sorrow in her eyes and he felt a sickening lurch in his gut—she wasn't a player. She was pinning everything on him and he'd really hurt her. He'd built this up, she'd been sucked in, and then he'd not even given her the time of day.

Even after five years the Achilles heel still gave him pain, this weeping sore of guilt that never dried up. He should be properly laying down the boundaries with Maria's brother instead of playing along, playing games with people like her.

She was too nice for this. Far too nice. She wasn't Maria...

'I see now,' he said, quietly. 'But it wasn't a case of "she'll do". You're more than that.'

He was saying words, walking down an avenue in the dark, not seeing where he was stepping, feeling his way along, and all of a sudden he'd arrived at a dead end. He had to stop wandering and turn around and say the words that were stoppered in his throat.

'I like you, Jacquelyn.'

It was as much a revelation to him as it was to her, but the moment the words left his lips he realised he meant them. And not just in the way a man commented on the temperature of the water in his whisky, liking it at room temperature, not chilled—he meant properly, thoroughly, the way he liked to taste the peat of the land, or the sherry of the casks, appreciating the layers and textures of the whisky itself.

'You *like* me?'

But he'd called it wrong again. Whatever she'd wanted to hear it wasn't that. Muscles were twitching on her face. Her eyes turned glassy but if she had opened her mouth and raged at him he couldn't have felt worse.

He reached his arms out but she hunched her shoulders.

'I do. I like you,' he said woodenly, confirming it to himself. He wanted to treat her well—not badly. He wanted her to like him too. And if her business was so important to her, he could make it up to her that way. He could step past his own rules and cut her some slack. It wouldn't cost anything other than a bit of back-pedalling and calling in some favours.

'I want to help you and all I was saying before is that Ariana's not right for House, but I know hundreds of other investors who might take you on, mentor schemes. Or work with an ideas agency. Rebrand. I can set that up today. Right now...'

He touched her, the bare skin of her arm above where she clutched herself, holding her elbows round her body like a shell.

'Come on. I know this seems like a disaster—but what have you got to lose?'

'You have no idea,' she whispered back.

Well, it seemed he'd done a lot of damage. A lot more than he'd realised, but he was trying to make up for it by offering her what he'd never offered anyone. He didn't do personal recommendations, and he didn't do pro bono work that was in any way directly related to House. He wanted… Dammit, he was completely determined now that she would benefit in some way from his business connections.

It was the least he could do.

'I have to head to New York. My accountant's waiting for me and I really can't put it off any longer. Come with me.'

As he said the words he was gripped by an enthusiasm that was so totally foreign to him. The thought of spending more time with Jacquelyn now was exactly what he wanted.

'I'll have it set up—we'll get you a day with the best people in New York.'

'No, no. Hang on. You're just saying words now. I'm not going to get on another plane with you for yet another waste of time.'

'It won't be a waste of time, Jacquelyn.'

'Really?' she scoffed. 'You really expect me to believe that?'

She should be biting his hand off instead of standing there stubborn as a mule, shaking her head. Didn't she know what she was being offered? This wasn't just a gimmick. This was real. This, he could deliver for her.

'Yes, I do.'

She almost laughed but he could see her falter a moment, a sliver of doubt reach her eyes, but then she recovered herself and stood there haughtily, regally, and it made him want her even more.

'So what's changed?' she said.

He levelled her a direct stare, he absorbed her face—the lips he'd kissed, the eyes that had flooded with unspilt tears—he saw arms that had held him and he wanted that warmth again. It had been absent for so long, so many years, and he wasn't going to deny himself any longer, not when he'd been offered it by a woman like her.

'I respect you. I respect that you called me on how I treated you. And the fact that you're still standing here. You came face-to-face with some pretty unpleasant people and you didn't flip out and run screaming. That says a lot.'

She stood a little taller. He saw it and it fed the sense that he was right, he could trust her.

'Just because I haven't run screaming doesn't mean I want any more of it. That's not why I signed up for this trip and I absolutely won't sign up for another where I'm likely to meet people like those two guys that were out there.'

'You're absolutely right,' he said quietly. 'And I am going to deal with it. It's been a long time coming but I can't live my life with this shadow hanging over me.'

'What are you going to do?' she asked, her clear blue eyes widening.

'I don't know yet. I can't turn him in. But I can't go on pretending that I don't know what he does. What he did. But don't worry,' he said, suddenly sensing her fear. 'Nothing will happen in New York. Nothing except the start of the next phase of Ariana.'

CHAPTER NINE

THE AIR-CONDITIONING WASHED OVER Jacquelyn's skin like a tide over pebbles as soon as she stepped inside the vast, gleaming Manhattan skyscraper. People bustled everywhere, a blur of confident strides and efficient handshakes, moving through the building and into elevators that flew skywards in glass caskets.

Jacquelyn stood beside Nikos, crushed so close she could see the tiny spiral of navy ink that peeped above his shirt collar, a tendril of the Sanskrit symbol that snaked over the back of his neck. She had been fascinated by it, kissed it, compared it to the others that covered various parts of his magnificent back and chest. But that was then—that night, never to be repeated. And this was now.

This was where she took every single chance that was offered to her and really made something of her business. This was the start of something wonderful. She was in a different league. Just being here made everything feel more possible. It was brighter, sharper, shinier, the people clear-eyed and confident. It was like the pixels of a perfect world, some computer-animated version of what the working week should really be like.

She tugged the cashmere cardigan over her shoulders, grateful for the hastily acquired luxury wardrobe that had been arranged for her—'an investment in your future', Nikos had said, dismissing her initial indignation at anyone offering charity, particularly when it involved making clothing choices on her behalf.

He was right. She couldn't arrive in Manhattan in a crushed sundress or a borrowed bikini. Instead she'd accepted the bags and boxes that were delivered on the plane and trailed her fingers through the best quality silk blouses in every colour. Cashmere cardigans and pencil skirts. Beige and patent heels, scarves and handbags. Lace underwear, lace-trimmed stockings. As someone who normally made her own clothes, she was completely spoilt for choice.

'I've got a lot to catch up on so I'll leave you with Lauren for most of the morning,' said Nikos as they walked along the moonstone carpets of his corporate suite, his eyes landing on everyone and theirs on him as he cut such a handsome dash in his slate-grey suit and pale blue shirt.

'Make every second count. Every person you meet will introduce you to another ten. At the very least you'll meet some people at the top of their game. You'll go back with a new strategy, a new look, a relaunch, and maybe suppliers, a designer, who knows…?'

He paused at a desk where an attractive young woman was sitting, and leaned his fingers on it. She looked up at him with an air of happy familiarity and Jacquelyn took a mental note.

'Any messages?' he said with a raised eyebrow, picking up the tablet the girl handed him and beginning to swipe.

'Oh, nothing really. You were AWOL for four days so, let's see, about four hundred.'

'Well within your capabilities, Lauren. Let me introduce you to Jacquelyn Jones. Your extraordinary organisational skills will be put to the test setting up her itinerary for the next few days. And adapting mine. I want Jacquelyn to come with me to the gala tomorrow evening and to dinner with Kostas.'

'I've already made a start,' said Lauren, flicking her eyes to the screen and then up to Jacquelyn. 'We have time with Monique on Madison Avenue.'

'Good choice,' said Nikos as he continued to absently flick through the electronic pad. 'What else?'

'This afternoon a VIP preview of the Bridal Exhibition and then a slot with the House Ideas people before dinner...'

Jacquelyn noticed that Lauren's voice trailed up questioningly and the pause that stilled Nikos's fingers as he swiped the screen.

'The House team? I would prefer Jacquelyn linked with an external agency. Try Cube. And for dinner, get a table at Joro—eight o'clock.'

'Of course. And a suite at...?'

He handed her the tablet.

'I've checked these. There's no sign of a meeting with Mark. Set that up for this morning. And no suite. Jacquelyn will stay with me, as my guest.'

With that he turned on his heel and walked off.

'Find Mark. I don't care where he is—I need to see him now.'

Jacquelyn was aware her mouth was open. So this was the CEO in his home environment, everybody scuttling about following his orders. Command and control. Well, not with her.

She *should* have had a conversation with him about their sleeping arrangements before now, and she couldn't very well shout *Separate bedrooms!* down the hallway after him. But as soon as she could, she'd tell him. There was no way she was going to let herself get into bed with him again.

With every passing hour she'd rued the moment she'd abandoned the principles that had kept her safe her whole life. Yes, she'd experienced pleasure like she'd never known, and she'd felt it deeply, too deeply. But to Nikos? It was just sex.

And maybe he wanted more; then he would have to find it elsewhere. She wasn't going to wring herself out all over again, she thought, turning back round to look at the efficient Lauren.

'Welcome to House,' the young woman said, turning on a megawatt smile and beaming up at her. 'We'll have your itinerary sorted within the hour.' She lifted the phone. 'Mark,' she said. 'Nikos wants to see you immediately.'

Lauren stood up, a perfect little pixie of health and vitality, and Jacquelyn felt an uncharacteristic stab of jealousy, wondering just how much of Nikos's life his personal assistant had access to.

'I'll take you to the Wellbeing Suite to wait.'

The hallway was screened off on one side with a sweep of cherrywood doors into which Nikos had disappeared, and glass on the other, through which she could see people in meetings, at desks, walking and talking, and that air of purposeful, happy busyness—the magic dust she'd longed to sprinkle in Ariana.

She'd already had to call Victor to tell him to focus only on the two made-to-measure orders they had waiting. She'd died inside, hearing the tone of disappointment in his voice when she'd told him she couldn't yet confirm what was going to happen to their collection, or to the team of seamstresses and machinists that worked for them, but they both knew that there was no money to cover their wages, not unless a miracle happened, and happened soon.

'Have you worked for Nikos for long?' Jacquelyn said, heaving herself back to the moment, as they walked back along the moonstone carpet.

'Four years. I met him when I was an undergrad at Athens University. He sponsors ten students every year and I was one of the lucky ones. I was offered an internship here while I got my MBA from Harvard. He's a fantastic boss. I couldn't wish for anyone better to work for.'

They'd stopped at the edge of a wide open lounge, where the shiny white doors of a sparkly kitchen area and large wooden table, beanbags and gym equipment announced themselves as the Wellbeing Suite. Vibrant citrus fruits were piled high in bowls, muffins and pastries sat alongside neat rows of bowls of berries and granola, and coffee filled the space with inviting scent.

'This is amazing,' said Jacquelyn. 'You can all help yourselves to this? Any time you like?'

'Yes—this is just for little breaks during the day. We have a full gym and a juice bar and café too. And of course access to all the perks that the House retail staff have. He thinks of everything.'

Jacquelyn looked around and thought of the poor girls who worked at the cutting factory in the out-of-town warehouse. They were so loyal to Ariana, when the heating had failed in the winter they'd worn fingerless gloves while she'd plugged in old electric fires for them, as they'd waited for the engineer. They'd work double shifts and go the extra mile every time she needed them. And now, if she didn't go home with good news, they wouldn't even have jobs.

'Yes, it is an amazing place to work. Although this is a first. I've never known him to do this kind of thing before. You must have made a very big impression.'

'I'm trying to save my business. I'll take all the help I can get,' she said, with steel in her voice that cut right through the happy little bubble that seemed to pervade every inch of the House International Head Office.

'You'll get the best from Nikos,' replied Lauren, smiling back sweetly. 'He's in a league of his own. It's the fact that he's willing to mentor a friend that's so unique. Honestly, it's great. It's the single thing that's drummed into us. There's personal, and there's business—but there's never both. No relationships, no favours for friends. Nada.'

'I'm not his friend,' she said, wondering herself what she was. 'I'm—'

'Oh, please—that is not my business. It's another line I don't cross.'

Jacquelyn opened her mouth to reply but her phone buzzed, and the call that she had been dreading lit up her screen.

'Hi, Dad,' she said, walking away from Lauren towards the bowl of gleaming oranges. She didn't need to check her watch to know that it was three in the afternoon in Marbella, that he would have been playing golf in the morning and he and Mum would be enjoying a snack on their terrace, reading the English newspapers and chatting about their dinner plans.

'Hello there, sweetheart. Just thought I'd give you a call to see how things are.'

Jacquelyn touched an orange, feeling the

bumps of the skin, imagining her father standing at the kitchen bench, her mother right beside him, the high sierra mountains and the bright blue sky behind.

'Oh, that's nice. How are you two? Is it still as hot? It's been weeks since we had a drop of rain. I'm beginning to wish for winter, already.'

She put the orange down and picked up some other fruit she didn't recognise. The fine hairs on its skin were foreign and strange as she rolled it around in her palm.

'Yes, it's hot here too. So how did it go, then? The Wedding Awards?'

'Same as ever. The food was very nice, but the band was different this year. Some new faces, but loads of people still there that you'd remember. I met Martin Lopez. He was asking after you. He's retiring soon too.'

'Is that right? Maybe he'll join me for a round of golf out here.'

'Maybe,' she said. She could hear the edge in his voice. He was biding his time to ask her.

'I heard Tim Brinley got an award. I hope nobody applauded.'

'He got an award and he tried to speak to me—to apologise. It's fine, Dad. I don't bear him any grudges.'

'He never did deserve you,' he said gruffly. 'And the Australian? He was there?'

There it came. His voice had weakened with age but there was no mistaking the sharpness of his intellect and Jacquelyn winced. It was only a matter of time before word got back to them that she had been seen with Nikos, or that she'd called Victor to say she was in New York.

'Yes, Nikos Karellis was there. He presented an award,' she said in a monotone voice, hoping for insouciance. 'Martin Lopez introduced us and we had a chat about the business. He was in the frame as a financier but it wasn't such a good match, Dad.'

When he didn't say anything she knew she wasn't going to get away with that. They probably knew other stuff too. Somebody could easily have seen her standing outside his suite after he'd had his shower. People were always jumping to conclusions.

'Did Barbara call?' she asked suddenly. She should know what she was up against at least.

'Yesterday afternoon,' he said.

'I see. And did she have anything interesting to say?'

'I think she's worried about you.'

'I wish she would mind her own business,' said Jacquelyn.

Her father didn't answer and the silent moment stretched by. She began to imagine the look on her mother's face as she listened to the gossipy phone call. The worry that would have crept over her brow, how her father would have gathered closer to the phone to try to listen in. How they'd probably talked about it all day wondering what to do, whether to call, whether to leave her alone. And then finally they'd decided.

'People only want the best, but it's your company now. You have all the big decisions to make.'

The first time he'd ever said those words the flush of excitement had made her feel high as a kite, flying in the air, weightless, exhilarated. Right now she felt worn down and weary, as if she were carrying rocks on her shoulders; every step was an effort.

'That's what I'm trying to do, Dad,' she said, injecting the solid, serious note she saved for these conversations into her voice.

She put the strange fruit back in the bowl and moved further to the side as someone came past to pour coffee. Some happy House International intern.

'And where are you now?'

She looked up. The Manhattan skyline could be seen through the panoramic windows. The industrious staff were all at work, here in their international headquarters. She felt like a goldfish in a bowl, staring at a world she could see but couldn't properly touch.

Her parents would never understand what she was hoping to achieve by being here. Every moment she was on the phone to them felt like air hissing from the punctured balloon of her ambitions. But there was no point in pretending.

'I'm in New York.'

She heard her mother's, 'Where did she say she was?'

And then his repetition, 'She says she's in New York.'

Her father was never angry with her. Never. She couldn't bear it. Letting them down was almost like a physical pain. When Tim had jilted her she'd been as unhappy for them as she'd been for herself—knowing that they were having to face the town and pretend that everything was all right.

It had crushed her, the shame. The guilt.

'Is this a holiday? May we ask who you are with?'

She stared down at her borrowed clothes, the pointed patent toes, at the pencil skirt and the exquisite blue silk shirt. What had seemed like a Cinderella nine-to-five wardrobe on the plane now felt silly and more than a little bit deluded.

What was she thinking, coming here to New York?

She held the phone to her ear as if she could muffle this world that she was standing in and keep it secret from her parents, keep them from knowing that she was here now because she had formed an unholy alliance with Nikos, an alliance that now involved this unwritten contract built on guilt and shame.

'It's not a holiday, no, but it's complicated. I'm on a business trip.'

She nodded, satisfied at that. It sounded feasible.

'You didn't say who you were with, Jacquelyn.'

She bit her lip.

'Is it Karellis?'

She nodded, just as a coffee was placed in front of her, as an arm rested lightly on her shoulder, as heat and strength and courage wrapped round her like a warm wind, but then as quickly were blown away as he lifted his arm and walked off.

'Yes. I'm at the House HQ, Dad,' she said, glancing after Nikos. He'd taken off his jacket. The blue sheen of his shirt glowed in the subtle low lighting of the kitchen. Her heart stuck in her throat as she watched him. The perfect proportions of his body, his long legs and wide shoulders, the cuffs of his shirt turned back once, exposing the strong bones and dark hairs of his wrists.

It was in every part of her—this feeling she felt for him. This was what happened when you slept with someone, she realised. This contract, this bond. He was her first and she would be linked to him for ever, even though he didn't know it. He was walking about oblivious and she was going to carry his face in her heart for ever. She had waited so long, built this up so much, and then in a single night it was gifted to Nikos and she was left with only a memory, not the lifetime of love that she'd always imagined would follow.

'What on earth are you doing there, Jacquelyn? If there wasn't any mileage talking to him at Maybury Hall, why pursue it in New York?'

A tear sprang up out of nowhere and she shook herself. The last thing she could afford to be right now was weak, in anyone's eyes. This was business, pure and simple. She swallowed.

'I'm going to meet some contacts that might be right for Ariana. House isn't right, as I said, but there are other opportunities that I'm here to chase up.'

Nikos had opened the fridge and stood illuminated in its blue light, as if he was searching for something, but she could tell he was listening. He took out a jug and poured a glass of carrot juice then reached for a muffin, moving with the graceful alertness of a panther.

'You need to go all the way to New York to find opportunities? Seems an awfully long way.'

'It's too good to pass up, Dad. But I'm only going to give it a day or so—if it doesn't feel right I'll be straight back to work.'

She wanted to glance at Nikos, to see how he reacted to those words, but she resisted, stared at her reflection in the glass instead.

'This isn't another wild goose chase, is it, Jacquelyn? Are you in a relationship with this man?'

She heard her mother's voice and then the phone was muffled, then passed over.

'Jacquelyn, it's me. Are you all right, love? Where are you? I'm worried about you.'

She glanced at Nikos. He'd put down the glass and stood facing her, his arms folded, staring at her intently.

'Mum, I'm twenty-five years old and I'm more than capable of looking after myself,' she said.

'But Barbara said you were with him, this Nikos. He's not your type, Jacquelyn. He's a ladykiller. He'll hurt you. I don't want to see you upset again, that's all. And he might promise you the earth but…'

'Oh, for goodness' sake, please stop worrying. I'm not in a relationship with him or anything like it. Nothing could be further from the truth.'

She turned to the glass and tried to say it quietly, throwing the words down to the carpet beside her shoes as if they might land there unheard. But when she looked up she knew that he'd heard them all right. The glass of carrot juice was sitting half-drunk at the counter, the muffin untouched and only the gleam of his shirt was visible as he walked back along the hallway. A shaft of light spilled out for a moment onto the carpet, and then was gone, as he disappeared inside a doorway, and closed it with a sharp click.

CHAPTER TEN

NIKOS DRUMMED HIS fingers on the table and looked up again at the inscrutable Mark.

'You're sure?'

'As I can be. The Inland Revenue still think you're laundering money. I've spoken to my guy and told him that we've got evidence it was Maria who invested in ghost companies, and that those companies have folded, but they're still sniffing. It's not what you want to hear, I know.'

'I want to hear whatever is going to get me out of this and let me get on with the rest of my life. I'd gift the whole damned lot to charity, every last cent of it—'

'If you only knew what there was to gift. I know. I get it.'

Nikos picked up the papers he had found in the safe again and looked at them, then tossed them down.

'So these are worthless? There was no point in me going to Greece to find them after all?'

'I wouldn't say they were worthless, no. But I think that they're probably only the tip of the iceberg. If you don't mind me saying, Mrs Karellis was a complicated lady with a big past. There's every chance she was involved in something like this.'

'But I can't believe I wouldn't spot it,' he said, shaking his head.

'You'd need to have been on her case twenty-four hours a day to keep up with her.'

'And I certainly wasn't doing that,' Nikos muttered to himself. 'If I needed anything to prove to me that business and pleasure don't mix…'

'You get a lot of pleasure from business, my friend. It's just certain types of pleasure that are better bedfellows with business than others.'

'You can say that again.'

Nikos checked his watch and looked up again at the smoky glass front of the restaurant. Jacquelyn was late. Knowing that was just adding to this list of stuff he had to deal with. He felt responsible for her.

He'd had a guard with her all day, and she was perfectly safe, but the nagging doubt at the back of his mind had got louder and louder, nearly drowning out all other thoughts.

Vital thoughts, like trying to pull memories

of Maria's businesses, any possible ways she could have hidden money.

When he'd first met her she had played a huge part in her first husband's businesses, because his illness had left her no other option. And she hadn't trusted anyone else.

But she'd been vague. What he'd put down to a lack of interest was more likely to have been a smokescreen. Always suspicious, always looking over her shoulder, and with good reason, because she'd always been up to something.

He racked his brains again. His first steps into business had been to cut through the mess that had been made with her first husband's businesses. She'd reassured him that she'd known what she was doing with her own money and he'd left it at that. He hadn't wanted to poke his nose in. He'd trusted her.

Had he? Had he really trusted her? He'd never checked her phone, followed her, gone through her things. She'd done all of that to him, had been insanely jealous when he'd spoken to other women. The times he'd stood there, absorbing her anger, her fury, sometimes even her blows. Because a man never hit a woman. As long as he lived he would never raise his hand to a woman, he would never be the man his father was.

That momentary flash of his mother's face formed again, the smile. She was so pretty, so Greek.

But it was those nights that he remembered most clearly. The roar of the motorbike engines in the distance, coming closer. Praying that it would go past the house but then hearing it stop; his father's footsteps on the path, the wooden boards that creaked as he listened to him climb, heavy footed, to the porch; straining to hear them over the sound of his own heartbeat.

The little prayers he would say over and over: *'Please don't make him angry...please keep Mum safe...please, God, take my pocket money and all my toys...'*

It always started hopefully, quietly. As if it might not actually happen, but then he'd hear voices, even muffled under his quilt, breathing in his own humid terrified air, he'd hear them, then the sound of her voice calling his name, letting him know she was all right, even as his father hit her.

'Are you OK?'

Nikos looked up.

'I'm sorry I'm so late, but I got a bit held up.'

Jacquelyn was standing right in front of him, a vision of blonde loveliness. He drank in the sight of her—the sunshine of her smile, the intense blue of her eyes, the roses on her cheeks shining with health and happiness. It was as if prison doors had opened into springtime.

'Hey, no problem. Grab a seat.'

He stood up and pulled out a chair, watching carefully as she slid herself down, pleased to see that she had chosen the blue silk dress that matched her eyes and showed off her slender arms and legs. And with a neckline that draped invitingly over her breasts, casting a shadow that his eye found pleasing. He felt an immediate stab of lust, and he did not, and would not, smother it.

She sat down and tucked her bag and briefcase on the other seat and looked up expectantly.

'Mark, this is Jacquelyn Jones. Mark is my accountant. We've just finished a meeting so you're right on time.'

'Oh, aren't you joining us for dinner?' she said, shaking Mark's hand. 'I'm really happy to sit and go through my notes. I've learned loads today and have been given some homework to do so I wouldn't be in your way.'

'No, Mark's leaving,' cut in Nikos. The last thing he wanted was anyone hanging around. He'd been looking forward to seeing her since he'd left her at the juice bar on the phone, denying that she was having a relationship with him.

It was interesting how hearing a few words could clarify a whole day's worth of doubt. Until that moment he hadn't known he really wanted a relationship with any woman but now he did. Even now when the timing was so off, especially now. And she had stood there denying him.

'Yes, I'd love to stay, but my boss here has other plans for me.'

'Put a team on this. Your best, most discreet people, but keep it in house.'

'It's lined up. I'll let you know how we get on.'

Nikos shook his hand. A hand he trusted.

'Are you sure you're all right?' asked Jacquelyn, sipping on water but looking at him. 'You looked shot when I came in. Was that bad news?'

'It's not great, but it'll be dealt with. It has to be.'

'Was it anything to do with the guys at the villa?'

He sat back and looked over her shoulder.

'You're doing that thing again,' she said. 'When you check out who's about. Like a secret agent. Not that I blame you.'

'Do I do that?'

'Since the day you picked me up to go to the airport.'

'I suppose I do.'

'A man like you, it's only to be expected. I guess there are always people on the make all around you, even if they only want to get their photo taken with you.'

'That's kind of you, but not every man like me has invited so much trouble into his life.'

'You can't help where you were born, or brought up.'

'No, but I can help who I choose or, rather, chose to marry.'

He didn't expect to feel the weight of those words as they landed but he did, and for a moment he was lost in a cloud of confusion. Marriage to Maria—had that really been him? It didn't just feel like a different life, it felt like a different man. He was so far away from there now he couldn't imagine making such a mistake again.

'I'm sure you'll make a very good choice,' she said quietly.

She dipped her eyes then, that sweep of lashes, such lovely lines that he'd grown accustomed to seeing now, that pleased him, and when she looked up at him again, her gaze was steady and sure.

'I can confidently say that I won't be making a choice like that again. Not when I see the mess it's got me into. Even five years after her death I'm having to pick up the pieces—if I can find the pieces.'

'I see,' she said.

'I'm talking in riddles, I know.'

'It's not my business.'

'Well, no, but you already know a lot of it. I was in Greece trying to find papers from an investment I knew she had, but it turns out she had some more. And we're not sure how she afforded some of the investments she made. Money has been going everywhere and the tax people want their share.'

'It can't be that hard to find. Somebody must know that there's money coming in and nobody is claiming it?'

'You'd think,' he said, musing on that idea for a minute. Somebody must be happily processing dividends into some bank account somewhere. It wasn't feasible that nobody knew what was going on.

'Is that why the guys were there? Have they got something to do with it?'

'That's what's worrying me. It isn't just blackmail.'

'Aren't you worried? Don't you think you should let the police know?'

'Involving the police is no guarantee this will get fixed. It might even get worse.'

'But you can't possibly think you can deal with all this on your own?'

Of course he was worried, of course he knew this was getting out of control. But letting the police know? It wasn't as simple as that. Things could backfire spectacularly. He had his dying mother to think about, his staff, even Jacquelyn. Innocent people became casualties in these kinds of wars.

The whole thing was so messed up.

'Anyway,' he said, keen to change the subject. 'How did you get on today? Tell me about your day.'

He tried to keep the tone light, tried to keep upbeat and interested. He was determined that Jacquelyn would feel that the trip was worthwhile, but he must not, would not, in any way get involved in this business, no matter how tiny, no matter how tempting it might be to make that face light up.

Because she was worth a lot of effort. He looked at her again and crushed down the urge to reach across the table for her, hold her hand and tug her towards him, and take a kiss from those lips.

'So yes, I couldn't believe it. The others were great but when I met Brody and he made me that offer, honestly I was blown away. I still am. I couldn't wait to get here and tell you.'

She was babbling with excitement, words pouring from her mouth, and he was just beginning to realise what she was saying.

'So Brody made you an offer? My friend Brody from Cube? Cube the digital marketing agency?'

He could feel something rise in his chest and he knew it was anger.

'Yes.'

She beamed. Her face was glowing and her eyes shining and it was some other guy who had done that. Brody—that creep from Cube.

'Literally less than an hour ago. It's—oh, my goodness—it is honestly the best. I couldn't have dreamed it. We'd met earlier in the afternoon at the Wedding Expo. He looked me out. Lauren had already told him that I would be coming later and he took such trouble to come and find me and talk to me.'

'I'll bet he did,' said Nikos, pouring water even though the waiter had just topped up their glasses. But he had to find something to do with his hands or he might rip something up, like the table.

'Yes. You know him? Of course you do. You set this up. I can't thank you enough.'

She moved as if she was going to reach

across the table and kiss him, but then she stopped herself. It was awkward, and he was now even more furious because it was as if Brody were sitting right there between them, on the table.

'You can thank me later—once I've heard what this amazing offer is.'

'He's going to be a backer. He has pots of money himself and funds people like me. I'm getting a million sterling and for that he only wants ten per cent.'

'Ten per cent of what? The business or the profits or both?'

'Well, the business, I think.'

'You haven't signed anything yet?' he said, suddenly aware that his anger was about to pour into curses just thinking about Brody. He should be happy for her, but he was in a rage that was hissing from his skin like steam. He had to keep a lid on himself, but he couldn't seem to dial it back down.

'Have you?' he repeated, unable to stifle the derision in his voice, which made him angrier again at himself.

'No. No, I haven't. Why?'

She sat back in the seat. Her shoulders slumped down. Her face sank and her eyes filled with concern. He felt like a piece of garbage.

'Do you think this is a bad move? It sounded so good. He was so positive.'

'Tell me exactly what happened.'

She looked around as if the answer were somewhere in the room full of people eating ridiculously expensive seafood, as if one of them were her witness and might help her out of this problem that had suddenly appeared, the storm cloud in her sunny sky.

'I met him at the expo. I told him why I was here…'

'Which was what? What did you tell him? Did you tell him that you and I…?'

She put her hand to her chest and looked hurt and horrified, and he caved, he honestly caved. He would do anything for this woman now, he realised. He would do anything and that idiotic creep Brody would be dust before he'd finished.

'No! Of course not. I would never tell any-one what happened.'

Her eyes had filled up. Silvery tears wob-bling on the lids of her eyes, pools he could dive into and not care if he drowned in them.

This time he reached for her hand, and held it in his own. He rubbed his fingers over hers, feeling the fine bones, the silken skin. He squeezed her hand. She didn't pull it away but she didn't meet his eyes and that hurt him.

'I already told you I regretted it so why would I tell anyone about it?'

She tugged her fingers away but he wouldn't let her. He leaned forward, touched her chin.

'I don't. I don't regret a single moment. I loved what we did. I only wish things were different between us, because I'd very much like to take you out. Properly.'

She looked up.

'I don't quite see how that can happen.'

'Things have a funny way of working out. I admit that I haven't covered myself in glory, but that doesn't mean I don't want to do better. I'm always trying to do better—in everything I do.'

'We all are,' she said. 'That's the reason I came here.'

He nodded. Part of him wanted to think that she'd come because of him but he'd blown it with his callous treatment of her. And he had a lot of making up to do.

'So, your new backer. Let's hear the rest of it.'

She sat back, composed again, but much less excited.

'I simply told him the story of Ariana. My grandmother, Dad, the Jones cut, how hard things are now. The competition from China. The made-to-measure clients that are so hard to come by, and how I'd called that wrong, expanding too quickly...'

She shrugged and his eyes swooned watching her. She was utterly perfect.

'And he offered you a million just like that?'

She sipped the wine that had just been poured.

'No. I told him I had been struggling to design. Since Tim.'

'You told Brody about your ex?'

Why is this hurting you? he chided himself.

Why should it bother him that she had confided in Brody about her ex when she would barely even acknowledge the guy's name when he'd raised it?

'Yes. I told him. I told him that my heart had been broken and that I lost control of what I was supposed to be doing. I had fallen in love with the idea of getting married and when it didn't work out I was stuck. I was stuck in a business where I was reminded every day that I'd failed. It was all I had wanted and I couldn't lift myself out. The business got into difficulties and I had to take over design again.'

'You told Brody all of that? And what did this look like? Was he taking advantage of you?'

The black rage was within him now. The

angry, jealous beast. The one that he had never allowed to so much as breathe inside him was now a dragon. The thought of sharp, brilliant, handsome Brody with his arm around Jacquelyn, patting her hair and soothing her with his *'There, there'* and waiting for his moment, the fox in the chicken coop.

Nikos had to get a grip of himself, he realised. He had to get back to couldn't-give-a-damn. Because he couldn't, or at least he shouldn't. Giving a damn was what had got him married to Maria in the first place.

Jacquelyn Jones was not his wife. She wasn't even his girlfriend. If she wanted to tell her sob story to some sharp-suited ex-lawyer-cum-financier, then tell it she should.

'He was a gentleman,' she said, with quite a heavy dose of indignation in her voice.

'Was he indeed? Good. Good that your new backer is a gentleman.'

She sat back properly now. 'You're jealous. I've just figured it out. You didn't want to get into business with me but you really don't want anyone else to either. Why are you doing this? Why can't you be happy for me? You were the one who set it up.'

'Jacquelyn, there is nobody happier for you than me right now. I am delighted for you. I just want to be sure that what you see with

Brody is what you get. I don't want you walking into a disaster and him walking away with half your business.'

She threw her napkin down now.

'You really have such a low opinion of me. I didn't realise it until now.'

He shook his head. 'No. I have a very high opinion of you. I just don't think that your business is…going the right direction.'

'Brody saw my problem straight away. He saw what I was trying to do and told me to focus on my designs.'

'Sure. Well, we already discussed that it was a designer that you needed only you couldn't afford one. You said yourself that your designs were your Achilles heel.'

'Not any more. Brody saw my new sketches. He thinks they're amazing.'

Now he knew he was on sure ground. The designs she had shown him were sterile, desperate, just not on the money at all.

'OK.' He put his hands up. 'If you're hearing what you want to hear and you don't want my advice…'

'My *new* sketches. I've done another four designs,' she said and her eyes were blazing again. Confidence dripped from the curl of her lashes, the ends of her fingers, the slant of her jaw as she sat back and tilted her head over the plate of crayfish that had just been served.

'I'd love to see them.'

She put her cutlery down and reached in her bag and pulled out her tablet without taking her eyes off him. The screen flashed to light and she quickly opened up a drawing app. Images popped onto the screen he immediately recognised as electronic sketches of wedding dresses. Vibrant, bold strokes, curving to create voluptuous, feminine figures. These were not at all like the ones he'd seen before.

'That's quite a departure from what you showed me last time.'

She nodded.

He flicked through the pages of each design, his eyes lighting up.

These were not the sterile aloof brides he'd expected. These brides were proud, and there was a confidence to the way they stood, hands on hips, facing fully forward.

'Wow, Jacquelyn. I'm impressed. You've taken this to a whole new level. These aren't talking "wedding day". These are talking "wedding night…honeymoon suite". Was that what you were after? Because that's what they're saying to me.'

He looked up. He could tell she was pleased, but pink dusted her cheeks.

'I didn't think so at the time but I see what you're saying.'

He was saying it all right. And he wanted to say it again, in person, now. He wanted to say it with every masculine part of his body. He wanted to imprint on her that he was the man who had made her sigh and cry and scream her passion in his arms. He was the best lover she had ever had, and, dammit, he was not going to give that crown to any other man.

It was no good. He threw down his napkin. He couldn't hold back any more.

'Have you had enough to eat?'

He was hungry—for her. He had to have her. His loins were full and aching and he was only going to get release one way.

She looked startled. He was going to have to manage this better, but somehow all his charm had walked out on him and all he had left was red-hot passion.

He put out his hand and urged her to her feet.

'Come on.'

'Don't you want to hear more about Brody and the deal?'

'That's the last thing I want to hear about. I want to talk about something else entirely.'

He was aware he was touching her, her elbow, her back, her waist, her hand. Possessive and unremitting, all the way through the crowded restaurant where people turned to stare, some of whom he knew, none of whom he wanted to speak to.

Out on the pavement and into the heat of the uptown evening, he stopped, arm around her waist now, checking up and down the street. The urgency with which he wanted to have her in private was tugging at him, it was the only thing he could think about, but he had to make sure there was no one around.

People milled past them, cars cruised and stopped, everything sluggish and hot, the day's heat still hanging over the city like a blanket.

'Let's walk. It's only three blocks.'

'To where?' she said, falling into step beside him. His hand tugged her closer, slid to her hip, felt the movement of muscle and bone through satin, felt his own lust kick in response.

She didn't pull away, she leant in closer and he knew with that single move that she was right there with him. She hooked her arm round his waist too and somehow a path appeared through the busy pavements. As if the universe and everyone in it seemed to know that they were lovers on their way to a night of passion and they were going to be rewarded, because it was beautiful. It was lovely. It was making love.

CHAPTER ELEVEN

THE RAILINGS OF what could only be Central Park stretched out ahead, a forest of iron slicing through grass and trees on one side, and dull grey concrete on the other.

Jacquelyn's heels clicked on the pavement, rattling faster than her heartbeat, signalling each new step on this whirlwind journey.

What on earth was going to happen next today? She'd woken up on a luxury jet, slipped into luxury clothes and cars, then meetings, dinner and now Nikos was steering her towards his apartment block, holding her to his side as if he was afraid the warm, gusty wind might blow her away.

All her wishes seemed to have been granted. Her dreams were coming true, one by one. Brody's offer was beyond anything she'd expected—it would solve everything. Salaries, rent, the lag time until next summer when the new orders would start paying.

And he was legitimate, she was sure of it. She didn't sense anything wrong, or creepy, just an honest-to-goodness interest in a traditional wedding dress design company and a belief in her ability, and her new sketches.

They were her best ever. That was the thing. Her hand had flown about as if possessed, as if somehow disconnected from her head, as if her heart or some other part of her was in control.

For the first time in her life her drawings felt alive.

Wedding night. Well, yes, maybe it was that. She knew now what it would have been like. She knew what other women knew, how their bodies would sing and their sensuality would be awakened by the touch of their lover, their husband. They wouldn't have awakened in the night alone and confused.

Nikos tightened his grip, holding her even closer, and her treacherous body swooned in response. She had to be careful. She couldn't let this get out of hand again. They could kiss, but she had to stop at that. She had to tell him.

'In here,' he said, guiding them into a tall apartment block, studded with elegant green awnings and guarded by a smart concierge, who doffed his cap as they strode right on through, past huge displays of white lilies and roses, a pretty East Asian receptionist, and into a plush, velvet-lined elevator.

Inside, and the doors slid slowly closed. Nikos reached across and pressed his thumb to the keypad. Immediately an artificial voice welcomed him by name. He ignored it, and stood back, stared straight ahead, expressionlessly. His arm was still around her but other than that he made no move to touch her.

'Are you all right?' she asked.

'Never better,' he said. 'Cameras.'

He nodded to the corner. The lift glided to a slow stop. A bell tinkled and the doors slid open into a light-flooded, parquet-floored vestibule.

'But there are none here,' he said and he tugged her hand and led her through the space.

She tried to see where she was, absorb her surroundings, this Park Avenue penthouse apartment, but Nikos spun her round in his arms. She felt his body, his strength, and her desire rose up like a flower hungry for sunshine and rain.

'Nikos, hang on. We need to talk about this,' she said, pushing herself out of his arms.

She put her hand up and walked backwards, stopping at a circular table that sat directly underneath a round cupola that flooded the space with light. Doors opened off in all directions, leading on through hallways dark with cherry reds and golds. She put her bag down on the smooth mahogany table, fumbling for the words she should say.

'Jacquelyn—you know I'm sorry about how I handled it. But I can't get you out of my mind.'

He walked up behind her and put his hands on her shoulders. She didn't pull away.

'You feel the same about me. I know you do,' he said, his voice quiet.

Slowly he let his arms slide around her, just holding her, cradled inside his embrace. He gently rocked her and she held his arms in place, loving the feeling, loving the way their bodies seemed to be so in tune.

Isn't this what you really want? To be in his arms again? Would it be so bad to have a kiss...?

He was so close, she let herself fall further back into his arms. Her body tentatively trusting that he was completely there, and he was.

'You know we have something special. This sort of thing doesn't happen very often. And I know I upset you but this time we'll play by your rules. Come on, Jacquelyn. Hmm?'

He bent forward, he nuzzled her neck, and just like that her body sang. She was almost ready to jump again. She could kiss him, she had to kiss him. She had to kiss him and then she had to stop…

'OK.' She turned around in his arms. 'But I'm not going to sleep with you,' she said. 'I want to make that clear.'

He pulled back, looked at her, his dark eyes glittering, his mouth curled into a smile.

'That's clear,' he said.

And then she grabbed his face, she cupped his jaw and pulled his mouth towards her. And for a moment they kissed, slowly, softly, but as soon as his tongue slid into her mouth she was lost. She knew that all she wanted was to go to that place where pleasure and love seemed to find each other.

'I've been aching to do this,' he said as they frantically grabbed at one another, his hands sliding over her dress, lifting her skirt, and she hooking her leg over his hip. He ground into her, crashing them back against a wall, as she held onto his shirt, laughing as she lost her footing, being scooped up and held fast.

'I haven't stopped thinking about you all day,' he said, and he slid his hands to her breasts, kneading them, weighing them, tugging at her nipples, already painfully hard, desperately proud and aching for his mouth. He tugged the neck of her dress down, ripping the fabric, exposing her nakedness underneath.

'You wore this dress knowing I was going to take it off you, didn't you?'

She threw her head back, clutched his head to her chest and held him there as he laved her with his tongue and teeth.

She had dressed with him in mind, of course she had. Everything she did was with him in mind. He lived in her mind, in her heart. He had got under her skin; every step she'd taken in this town she'd imagined sharing with him. It was hard to remember that she'd known a world empty of Nikos, when he filled it now so completely.

'I've never wanted a woman so much. Touch me,' he said. Her fingers flew to his belt, his zip, the hard, hot force of his erection. She longed to see and touch and taste and feel him inside her.

His breath was coming in short panting bursts, between each clever touch.

'We are going to have another night to remember, Jacquelyn.'

He pulled her closer still.

Another night like her first. The discovery of love, the heights of passion and the novelty of masculinity, but not just anyone's masculinity—Nikos, her first ever lover. The man whom she'd always hold in her heart.

'All night long.'

'You won't get up and leave me in the middle of the night this time?'

'No. You're my guest here. I'm not going to do that,' he said.

His guest.

Was that all she was to him? A house guest, here today, gone tomorrow?

What if there was no tomorrow? What if she was just filling his nights the way Lauren filled his days? Was she just the disposable blonde from England who happened to fall into bed with him whenever he clicked his fingers? No matter how she looked at it, she wasn't his equal in this. It was his apartment, and these were his terms.

And she was worth more than this. She was from a family where love was not throwaway. It was for ever—and she wanted a for-ever love.

With strength that came from somewhere deep inside, she pulled herself out of his arms.

'No,' she whispered. 'No, no, no. I don't want to be your *guest.*'

He stood there, exposed, his erection straining forward, his shirt tugged open, his face stained with lipstick and his eyes wild with disbelief.

'What's the problem?' he said.

'I want to know what I am to you,' she said, quietly.

'Jacquelyn,' he said, but she couldn't look at him. 'What do you want me to say? You're staying here with me for a few days, as my guest. I don't get what the problem is.'

'I'm sorry, no. I can't do this.'

'Why? What's happened?'

She straightened her dress, and turned away from him, fixing herself as best she could, stopping the tears with sheer willpower as they pooled in her eyes. She breathed deeply and, with a sigh that came from the pit of her stomach, she shook her head and walked away.

'I'm sorry, but no. This isn't right. It's not who I am.'

How did she explain this to him? How could she tell him that she felt so strongly that making love was so much more than a fun way to spend an evening?

It was huge, bigger even than she had ever suspected. Since she'd taken Nikos to her bed, she'd given away part of herself and she felt the weight of her decision so deeply.

She looked back but he was still standing where she'd left him, his face a mask of disbelief. How could she say any of this to him when she was just another woman in his bed?

'Would you mind telling me what's going on?'

She looked blankly around. The apartment

was exactly as she had imagined it. The walls a dark burgundy, vintage furniture, brass and mirrors from a more elegant age. Statuettes of long-limbed women with short hair holding glass shades, twenties icons, art deco, beautiful.

She clutched her arms around her body, protecting herself from the fierce blast of his maleness, in case she succumbed again, because she did so want to. She had to distance herself from this, put some space between them, calm it all down, pour ice on the heat.

'I shouldn't have come here,' she said.

He stared, incredulous.

'Look, I know it looks as if I've led you on, but I—I can't explain.'

'I wish you'd try, Jacquelyn. I really thought we were on the same page here.'

Why was this so unfair? Why couldn't Nikos be hers? Why, when she had finally found him, was he so unavailable in the way that really mattered? He was everything to her, she would never meet another like him, and it broke her heart that there was no future for them.

She felt tears form and her head hung and then he was there as his arms slid back around her. Close and closer they stood, hugging and holding one another under the cool stares of his art deco sculptures. Through the damp linen of his shirt she scented him, learned the slow steady beat of his heart, let the rhythms of her body and breath settle and synchronise with his.

He was a rock, a solid, kind, stable man. A good man. But he wasn't her husband and he wasn't even her lover. She was just one of many and then she'd be gone, and he'd always have a part of her and she'd only have this part of him, and it hurt her so badly to know it.

It was a bond that was deep, vast, endless. She felt it with every steady beat of their hearts, but he was miles away from where she was.

'I'm the one who is sorry now,' she said finally, peeling herself back from him. 'I owe you an explanation. But it's hard for me. I don't think like other people.'

'Let's sit down and talk about this.'

In the sleek, modern kitchen he made tea as she eased herself onto a chair. The reassuring sights of water filling a kettle, cupboards being opened, mugs produced, soothed and settled her. It was lovely to watch Nikos's masculinity in such simple, domestic tasks.

He would have been a good husband, she thought. There was no bitterness in her heart; she wouldn't allow it.

'You know your way around this place a lot better than the last kitchen we were in.'

'I can make tea in any country. Bear that in mind,' he said, brandishing a teaspoon. He was trying to lighten the mood, she could tell that, but it was an empty laugh she returned and it echoed around the kitchen, hollow and cold.

'How long have you lived here?' she asked, noting the collection of books that were piled on the table, management and leadership titles, bookmarks poking out. Under a shaft of light in the hallway, photographs of Nikos with some of his very famous and less famous friends. She strained her eyes, noting that Brody was among them.

'Seven years,' he said, wearily, as he settled a mug of tea down in front of her. She clasped her fingers around it, glad of the heat it brought. 'I bought it when I was going through a rough patch with Maria. That's not to say that every other patch was smooth—they were all bumpy one way or another. That time was one of the worst.'

'Was she unfaithful?'

She asked it carefully. Her opinion of the woman wasn't great, but to think she could have deliberately hurt Nikos was awful. Infidelity was as painful as being jilted, she supposed.

He raised his eyebrows and laughed mirthlessly, and she knew she was right.

'Let's keep tonight to the present. You were going to tell me what happened back there.'

'I...' she began. How to find the words? How to say this without looking like a complete fraud? She should have told him before now. She should have told him that she had once believed in something so deeply that she had cherished it until the safety of it had become more important than what it stood for. How she had never, ever before been so swept away that her lifetime promise had felt meaningless. How she had let it go like opening her hand on a breezy day and letting a precious flower be blown away by a gust of wind.

She knew he wouldn't understand her either; nobody did. But she had no other truth to tell.

'I don't believe in sex before marriage.'

He was leaning against the kitchen worktop, handsome, virile and strong, looking godlike, as he always did. The only sign that he'd even heard her was the surprised hitch of one jet-black eyebrow.

'OK. That's not what I expected to hear. So if that's what you believe, why did you sleep with me?' he said. 'You can't honestly think it was going to lead directly to a proposal?'

'Of course not,' she said, blushing furiously.

'Just checking,' he said. 'It's different, but it

wouldn't be the first time a woman has asked me to marry her.'

'You're completely misinterpreting what I said,' she said, putting her tea down a little too vigorously.

'Tell me, what does us having great sex have to do with a lifetime commitment? I've lived that particular nightmare already, remember? I've lived it and I'm still reliving it. It's still haunting me. She might be dead but the ties are still choking me. And there's no way, none, that I'm ever going near that again.'

'I'm not asking you to marry me!' she said as anger bubbled right up and over. He was insulting her, choosing to totally misunderstand her, just because he didn't want to lose face.

'Maybe not, but I'm feeling manipulated here. We had a great night together. Why do we need to wrap it up as something it's not? I barely even know you, Jacquelyn. I promised myself I was never going to get into one of these scenes again so, trust me, I'm not the marrying type. Not any more.'

She stood up, pushed herself back from the table, stared at him.

'I—'

'I,' he said, silencing her, 'was asking you to go on a date, with a view to going on another, you know, the way people do, gradually getting to know one another.'

Yes, she wanted to yell, and that was the problem. They should never have done what they'd done. She should never have succumbed.

'Why don't you take that as a compliment? Or are you planning to give me the "bitterly regret it" line again? It only works once. Or at least, it only works once with me. How many other times have you used it?'

'I've never used it,' she said, her voice shaking over the huge hot lump that formed in her throat. The thought of being wrongly accused was always awful, but to be wrongly accused over something like this was beyond the pale. It pierced her, it cut her, and she had no weapon to fight back with, other than the truth.

'I was a virgin. You are the first man I ever slept with. And you have no idea how deep my bitterness goes. None.'

She couldn't see his face because she was staring at the pile of his stupid books, straining so hard not to bleed from the hurt of this awful conversation.

'A virgin?' he repeated, as if she'd said 'an alien' or 'a unicorn' or something equally unusual. 'A virgin? But I asked you. I knew there was something going on and I asked you.'

She didn't look up from the mug of tea in

front of her, now glassy and opaque with un-shed tears, but she could tell he was walking about the kitchen and she waited to hear him, waited to hear what he would say.

'What am I supposed to do now?'

She shook her head and crushed her eyes through the glassy tears, forcing them to dis-appear. So that was it. That was how he took the news. The secret and all that it meant to her was just a 'thing' to him. This was even worse than she'd imagined. He was so callous. What a fool she'd been.

She shook her head and pushed herself up from the table. She didn't need to prolong this. The faintest tiny flicker of hope that something might linger and grow was completely doused, ashes cold in a grate.

Everybody does it these days. There is no shame—none...zero—in having sex. There is much more shame in not having it.

She'd thought about that so many times. Her needs were romantic and spiritual. They were lifelong, enduring and deep as the widest, blu-est ocean. There was nothing throwaway about anything she offered and nothing she could do would ever change that.

The awful thing was she'd traded that one single night for all the nights that would come after.

'Where are you going?'

'Away from here.'

'I'm sorry if you're not getting the reaction you want but if you'd told me at the time I would have handled things differently.'

'It's not the kind of thing I go around broadcasting.'

'Maybe you should. Because any man taking a virgin to bed needs to know that stuff.'

'My body is my business.'

'You're smarter than that, Jacquelyn. You're the one who's held on for twenty-five years. You were engaged to some guy, for God's sake. What the hell happened there that you chose to sleep with me and not him?'

'Just leave me alone. The last thing I want is a post-mortem.'

'No, but I do. You're the one who's been holding all the cards and you've just landed this on me. Look, sit down. I'm not going to let you go anywhere so let's get that straight.'

She stopped in the doorway, her back to him; the beaming smiles of politicians and movie stars gazed at her from photographs on the wall. She searched for the photograph of Brody and wondered with a lurch of panic if Nikos would get in touch with him over this, if it would somehow sour things.

'OK,' she said, lifting her jaw and turning

around. 'Maybe I should have told you, but I didn't. I didn't think it was anyone's business but mine, so if I have upset you I apologise.'

'You don't look or sound the slightest bit sorry. Actually, you look angry. With me. As if I'm the one who's done something wrong.'

'I'm not angry. I'm just so disappointed,' she said. 'I had my own rules and I broke them, and I've got to live with myself.'

'Hang on, I think I'm working this out— you actually think that there are rules around this sort of stuff? You need to sign a licence or wear a piece of metal on your finger? Making love isn't about rules, it's about people. It's about chemistry. The fact that you didn't make love until you were twenty-five is because you didn't meet anyone that turned you on enough.

'And then I came along. And suddenly you felt real chemistry. Just like I did. And just like I did you gave in, you followed your instincts. And your instincts were proved right because we fit. We work. On a physical level we work. But that doesn't fit with your plan because in your world of unicorns and fairies, your handsome prince is supposed to marry you first and then you have babies and live happily ever after.

'But life isn't like that. Marriage isn't like that. Marriage is hard work. It's making the best of a goddamned terrible life. It's waking up one morning and seeing your glamorous new wife for what she really is. It's coming home from work one night and finding her naked in the hot tub with another man.'

He threw his head back, bunched his hands in fists and shook them at the ceiling, hissed curses. Then he spun round, and the look blazing from his eyes was awful. He looked tortured, a soul bound in some dark, desperate hell that he could never escape.

'*That's* marriage. And that's what I will never do again. OK?'

'I'm so sorry for you,' she said, hearing those words as if they were rocks he'd flung at her, flinching with every blow. 'I don't know what you lived through and I'm glad I never will, but your experience is unique to you. It doesn't mean that mine or anyone else's will be the same.'

He shook his head; he'd turned away, defeat in every muscle, every movement of his magnificent body. She sensed it from him and she wanted to wring it out of him like water from a cloth, but there was no point any more—he had moved so far away from her, so far from that place where they'd shared something and could build on it, to a place buried beneath walls of guilt and shame and his own dreadful past.

'Yeah, well, your experience is a bit limited, if you don't mind me saying.'

He poured a glass of water and drank thirstily.

'Not every experience has to be lived firsthand. I saw the marriage of my parents, every day until they moved to Spain. And it wasn't perfect, but it was good. They were solid. Not everyone lies and cheats, Nikos.'

'No, and I don't suppose every wife has to be beaten until she haemorrhages either, but some do, and there's nothing anyone can do about that either,' he said, walking past her back into the hallway. 'I need a drink.'

She stood watching him disappear through a huge doorway. The Beast in his castle, howling with pain and unable to see the light in the world.

She had known pain, but not like his. Not pain so deep it had seeped into the air in his lungs, the blood in his veins. Nobody could leave any creature in pain like that, no matter what he had done or how he had treated her. No matter that she was alone in an unfamiliar apartment in an unfamiliar city with no friends and nowhere to go, completely beholden to this man for his kindness, and dependent on him for a roof over her head, and business contacts and a way out of debt to save her business.

No matter that he was so far gone he'd forgotten she was even here.

She had to do something.

Clicking fiercely along the parquet, she followed him, rounding the massive doorway and entering the room. For a moment she struggled to see him, so vast was the space.

Huge gilt mirrors towered over sleek furniture, all of it way out of her income bracket. A marble fireplace as big as her shopfront, its grate like the mouth of a cave, sat centrally under an oil painting that was surely a Picasso. Windows like skyscrapers opened onto the darkest night sky and the myriad lights of the New York skyline.

It was breathtaking, and there was Nikos, in the corner, turning on lamps and lifting a bottle of amber liquid from a silvery tray. She heard the soft pop of a cork as he started to pour it into a glass. He filled it half-full and lifted it straight to his mouth.

It was an act of self-destruction and it frightened her.

'Not even going to add water?' she heard herself cry.

He paused, but only for a second before he threw it down his throat.

'Oh, I bet that feels better now. Just what you need. Get yourself legless. Anything to drown out the drama that this pain in the backside has brought to your door. Poor you.'

He poured another and put it to his lips, but then turned and stared at her.

'You've got a problem with my drinking now?'

'No. You're the one with all the problems, remember?'

He swilled the whisky around his glass, looking at it as if it was his enemy and he was going to take it head-on.

'That's right, sweetheart, they just keep on coming.'

'You're not the only one in pain around here,' she cried. 'Plenty of people have difficult marriages and hurt each other. But I thought more of you than this.'

'Save the sermon. You don't know what you're talking about.'

'Look at what you've built. Look around you. This was all you. House is your creation, and you're…kind, you're a good man. You were a great husband. And you've given me a chance here—and I know I won't have been the first one. Nikos, stop doing this to yourself and listen.'

His eyes had darted from the glass to a mirror where she could see in the reflection that he was watching her. A hall of mirrors, all reflecting this same dreadful scene.

'Forget it. You're wasting your breath.'

He lifted the glass to his mouth again but this time she couldn't stand it.

'Stop all this self-pity. Just stop it!'

She stormed across the room, her heels sinking into the heavy oriental rug, slowing her down, but she wouldn't be put off and she reached him, reached the glass and yanked it out of his hand.

As quickly he grabbed her arm and the whisky sloshed over her hand and down her arm. Drops landed on her face, her lips, and some on her chest.

His face was blazing, and his grip was unremitting. They stood, like a still life, a cartoon scene of power and anger and beauty, completely still apart from their panting chests and the hard, fast breaths that sounded from their noses and mouths.

He was magnificent, and intimidating, but she would not back down. She stood tall and faced him toe to toe, focusing on his blazing dark eyes, his high stained cheekbones, and tense, square jaw. His lips, when she looked there, had softened, parted.

But it was his presence that undid her. His brooding, masculine presence, close, so close

and so magnetic she was utterly compelled to
let her guard drop and sink into his space.

And then desire flooded her whole body.
She felt it rise like a tide, flushing into her
most sensitive parts, weakening her mind, her
resolve, her fight.

'What do you suggest we do now, Jacquelyn?' he hissed. 'Are you going to give me another lecture on self-love or do we rip each
other's clothes off and make love? Do I take
your body the way I did the last time? My God,
you're so ready for me, look at you.'

He dropped her arm but he spun her round
until they were both facing one of the mirrors.
He stood right behind her, holding her arms
down by her sides, the splashes of the whisky
clearly marked on her dress, one nipple bold
like a stud under the damp satin. Her cheeks
were pink, her lips were open, her hair was
tousled and trailing her shoulders.

She looked wanton.

Behind her, she saw his dark jaw and short
dark hair, the inked tattoos of his muscled arm
and bare chest exposed, the sheer breadth of
him surrounding her, and behind them the op-
ulence of the room, huge, lofty, elegant, im-
mutable.

'Tell me and I'll do it.'

Her head fell back, she longed for his touch,

she willed his hands to move, to mould her, his lips to kiss her, his tongue to lick her. She yearned with every fibre of her being to have that night again.

She could feel the heat, the strength, the force of him, hard and desperate, and she knew that he was her lover, she could be his lover again, rolling in his arms, showering him with her kisses, feeling those strong limbs entwined with hers, feeling complete, and whole. Feeling that she was a *woman*.

'Mmm… Jacquelyn,' he whispered, softening, drawing her further into his space. Her neck was extended now, her whole body throbbing with desire. In the mirror she saw his head bend towards her, his lips close to her ear, and a shudder loosened itself and reverberated from her neck to her core to her very fingertips and the sensitive buds of her nipples.

She opened her eyes wide, watching. How wonderful they looked together, she in the sleeveless blue satin and he in his slate-grey trousers and pale blue shirt. She was the woman in her sketches. He, the groom of her dreams.

Almost. But that wasn't real; they weren't that couple. They were two single people alone in New York. And tonight there would be love but what would there be tomorrow?

Regret. Pain. Guilt, when she finally, in however many months or years, stood next to her real husband, whoever he may be, promising that she would love him for ever, but knowing that she hadn't waited for him, that she had given in to temptation and bedded Nikos again, broken her vow, not just once, but twice.

He wasn't going to change. He'd been as plain as he could be. He was never going to settle down, or fall in love with anyone again, not in the way she needed to be loved. If she slept with him now, she'd lose him for ever.

And she'd been as plain as she could be. There was no compromise. No winner or loser. Nothing for either of them to gain but another night of memories.

How could she live with herself?

She closed her eyes, and shook her head, and with a force of will that felt as if she were moving the earth itself she pushed herself away.

'No,' she said.

Yes, screamed her body. But she shook her head and prayed that he would listen.

'No,' she said again. 'It's not who I am. I can't do this again.'

He moved away, just a fraction of an inch, and in the chasm of silence that stretched now between them she bowed her head and heard the steady tick of a clock, each second moving on in time, past this moment.

It hit the hour and chimed ten long beats.

Like a spell broken, she stepped back onto the rug, sank down on the silk cushions of a hard, high sofa. She was safe. She was back on solid ground.

He sat opposite her, his head in his hands. The long, strong fingers cradled his head, tufts of black hair poking through and the snake of ink disappearing down his forearm.

She stared at him, and such a pain, a physical pain of loss and longing, pierced her that tears sprang in her eyes and she wiped them away. If she stayed a moment longer she would want him so badly that she wouldn't be able to stop. She had to get away.

'Nikos. Can you call me a cab?'

After a few moments he sat up, shook his head. His eyes were dark, unfocused.

'Sure. Whatever you want. Where do you want to go?'

She didn't know. She truly didn't know.

'Home,' was all she could think of to say.

He looked sharply at her now.

'When you've come all this way? You're nearly there. Stay on. Finalise things with Brody.'

'You won't pull the plug on that?'

'I'm a bastard, Jacquelyn, but I'm not that much of a bastard.'

He sighed, long and slow, and in every particle she could hear how exhausted he was.

'I've got things to take care of. I'll be heading back to Greece tonight. I'll make arrangements for a hotel; my car's downstairs. Lauren will take care of everything for you.'

'I can't go to a hotel. I don't have any money.'

A look passed over his eyes, fleeting and final. He nodded. 'You won't need any. You're here now. You've arrived. Things are going to work out for you. I'll take care of the short term.'

He stood up, and she stood up.

They faced each other for the second time, and she stretched out her hand to shake his, businesslike, just how it should be.

'Come on,' he said, shaking his head. 'We're more than that. Way more than that. You don't need to worry. You've drawn your line and I'll respect that.'

He nodded behind him to the space they'd just stood in.

'That won't ever happen again.'

She glanced there and it was as if she could still see that version of Nikos and Jacquelyn, crushed together and loving one another. The way her life would have unfolded if she'd only let it happen.

'Jacquelyn, I would never put you in a position you didn't want to be in, you can be sure of that.'

'Maybe we could date?'

She heard the words escape her mouth— desperate, begging, a last-ditch attempt at staying in his life—and cursed herself.

'We could. But you want to be married. And I don't want to feel responsible for anyone else for the rest of my life. I'm not very good at it.'

He turned on his heel, and walked back through the vast room, picking up his keys and his jacket. He lifted her bag where she'd dropped it and handed it to her, walked to the elevator and it opened immediately.

'I'll see you downstairs.'

She didn't argue, because these were the last few moments she would have with him, possibly ever. Her last supper, those gulps of air, the intoxicating joy of being with Nikos were soon to be gone, and she knew that more and more painfully with each passing second.

As if she were walking to her own execution she followed him downstairs and back through the cavernous lobby. The concierge lifted her face in a smile and dipped it back to her screen. The lilies, proud and beautiful in their square vase, the gleam of the cherrywood table and the wide cold mouth of the fireplace—all still there, as they had been less than an hour earlier.

Nothing had changed except them. Life moved on.

On the pavement outside, his car waited just beyond the green carpet, its windows reflecting this man and this woman, and this parting.

Nikos smiled and put out his hand to her, then stepped towards her and wrapped his arms around her, surely and confidently, and she felt the tremors of terror build. Panic began to creep over her. She wrapped herself around him, tighter and tighter.

Please don't go, don't leave me, she whispered to herself.

He held her, unmoving, solid and still.

'Shh…' he whispered. 'You'll be fine.'

He knew.

There in the power of his body she slowly began to quieten and they held each other, like friends, like long-lost friends who'd found each other and who knew they must say goodbye again. For ever.

CHAPTER TWELVE

SUMMER ROLLED BRIGHT and warm, like a cheerful carpet of colour, all the way down Fifth Avenue. Here and there yellow cabs and cars cruised and paused patiently at lights. It was early, it was quiet, but Jacquelyn could feel the energy build, like an audience taking its place in a theatre, just before curtain up.

She had three more blocks to walk in heels that were better suited to office floors than pavements. She eyed the trainers of other women who were already making their way to work, fast, efficient, appropriate.

If she stayed on here that would be what she would do, but in two days' time she would be heading back to Lower Linton, back to her studio and to Victor, to the girls in the workshop, finally able to share the good news.

It was the best present of all, and had managed to eclipse some of her sorrow. Her morning mask was truly in place but her eyes were puffy and her mouth pinched. She'd positioned it over and over into the deceitful smile, trying so hard to stop her mind drifting off into hopelessness.

Her business was her husband. That was how it would be. She had been offered this union and she would make it work, for all of them, and she would force her face into that smile all day long if she had to. Because she had the nights to cry into her pillow.

Her heels rubbed again and part of her was glad of the extra pain. It seemed to amplify her suffering even more. But she couldn't afford to get a blister, not with a full day of meetings, lunch and dinner. Brody had taken her schedule from Lauren now and between them they had remodelled it into another series of amazing opportunities. In two days every single worry had been obliterated. Everything except Nikos.

As well as the investment, her new designs were incredible. More than Brody had taken notice; she was in talks to make couture and occasionwear too, with the buyer from one of Nikos's biggest rivals. They were going to run her designs in the biggest stores in the States, Canada and Australia.

And she couldn't stop designing. Her Achilles heel had been repaired and become her engine. Her pen was flying, her designs improving, refining. These women that she sketched now had bodies and felt pleasure behind their blank faces. There was a completeness that had never been there before, an understanding of what it was to be a woman.

She knew she was drawing herself. She wasn't that stupid. She knew it was her way of pretending that her fairy tale was still unravelling to its joyful conclusion, the woman she was now, the bride she was going to be. The last thing she could do was stop to remind herself that the major part of her fairy tale missing was the handsome prince.

No, those thoughts were for the darkness of night, the pillow soaked with tears and the emptiness of her bed, the misery of another day dawning, cold and all alone. The woman who designed wedding dresses she knew she would never wear. Because she couldn't have Nikos.

Her eyes burned again. There was no time for this now. She had to keep on this treadmill, keep focused, keep going, until she got back to Lower Linton and could finally close the door on the world for a while.

She paused at a junction. Her heel throbbed as she waited with the other pedestrians for the Walk sign to change. At the corner of her eye, a limo rolled by, more slowly than the others. So much money in this part of the world, on this street. Luxury everywhere she looked.

The crossing sign changed and she stepped out, caught in the crush of people moving. She checked the street signs, noting the numbers, counting where she should be. Two more blocks to go. Brody would be waiting. He'd offered to send his car but she'd wanted to walk. Another stupid mistake. This blister was sending darts of pain along her foot; every step hurt.

And it was getting busier now. A woman stepped out in front, she adjusted her path; a man appeared at the side, a car parked right next to the kerb, she had no room to move and was bumped, stumbling into someone else's path.

'Sorry,' she muttered, trying to right her steps, but somehow she couldn't rebalance, somehow she was heading further off to the side, dragged by the flow of people.

But then a car door opened and she seemed to be falling towards it.

'No,' she tried to say, 'this isn't my car,' but hands grabbed her and she was shoved right inside, falling on her knees. Her shoe loosened, the door closed, the car moved.

'No!' she said again, pulling herself up from

the carpet to the leather seat. The car turned sharply, throwing her across it to the other door. She lunged for the handle, desperately feeling for a button to click, but there was none—just smooth plastic. Panic doubled with every missing lever on the door, the window, but no matter how much she grasped, there were no buttons, no escape.

Frantically she battered her fists against the smoky glass. People passed by, legs moving, heads forward, oblivious.

'No, you don't,' came a voice behind her. Gruff, Australian.

Arms circled her waist and heaved her onto the seat. She tried to push back up but huge fingers curled round her shoulders, shoving her down.

'Sit down. And shut up.'

She sank back in the seat, shrinking away from him, this dark malevolent presence, this strong, terrifying man, but she knew who he was, even as her mind tried to make sense of this, and grasped for reasons why, and how wrong this was, what a mistake.

'You're Nikos's father.' She gasped, daring to look at him.

'Ten out of ten.'

He sat back beside her and she scuttled along the seat, away from him to the door, staring out of the corner of her eye. He didn't move, stared straight ahead. His face weathered, and coarse, his head shaved, he was every bit as brutal as she'd imagined.

'I'm nothing to do with him. I'm not his girlfriend.'

'I told you to shut up, Blondie.'

And then he reached over and grabbed her hair, tugging her neck back, and a sharp pain lanced her. She cried out but he tugged tighter.

'How much further, Bruno?' he said, over her scream. Then he tugged again until she realised that with every sound he tightened his grip. She had to swallow the pain, and her scream, and then when she was silent, save for her breath and her feet scraping on the floor, he let her go with a shove.

'It works like this. Quiet—no pain. Noise— pain. You got it?'

He lifted his hand as if he was going to strike her. She flinched, then nodded and scuttled even further into the corner, pulling her legs up and hugging herself into as tiny a ball as she could. There was a driver in front, the doors were locked, the car was rolling through Manhattan, and she was terrified for her life.

Central Park appeared. The railings, the awnings, Nikos's apartment block.

'That's it,' he said, leaning forward to the driver. 'Circle the block and then pull up.'

He looked over at Jacquelyn and there in that look she saw Nikos. She saw his eyes and his jaw. She saw the shape of his head and the stretch of his shoulders. She saw his power and might and the strength that had driven him to greatness, but here in his father all that power had turned into evil and terror, and she shuddered to think what he would have been like as a father. How brutal.

Poor Nikos. And his poor mother. Her heart broke to think of them.

'How much longer?' he asked the driver, who shrugged his shoulders.

The car had rounded the block and now rolled to a stop and parked, well back from the entrance.

'I don't know. Ten, maybe.'

'OK, Blondie. Your turn. Time to call your little sweetheart.'

Nikos tossed his mobile phone down on the sofa and walked out onto the terrace. The magnificent panorama across the park and beyond had been one of this apartment's selling points. It wasn't unique. There were loads of great spaces on Fifth Avenue that he could have had, still could, but this place had grandeur and elegance, and it was isolated. It was impossible to break into and after the burglary at the villa it had been a weight off his mind to know that, no matter where he was in the world, this little slice of Manhattan was safe.

But now that the dragon was out of his lair, nowhere was safe any more.

He was still coming to terms with what he'd found out these past days. The investigators had tracked down Maria's old maid, and, just as he'd predicted, she had delivered up the news.

He was shocked, but not that shocked. Maybe because he'd always suspected his old man had been behind the break-in at the villa, and maybe that was why he had refused the police offers of help. Any path that led back to Arthur was a path he wasn't prepared to take. Even if his father was stealing from him. Even if he'd been naked in a tub with his wife. Nikos had walked away that night, too full of dread at starting something he couldn't control. It was easier to 'turn the other cheek'. Or be a *pathetic little girl'*. Those words had been flung at his back, his father's daggers hitting home.

He hung his head, sickened at the thought, but it was the truth. The ugly truth that his father was untouchable, protected by his own wall of fear, his henchmen like gargoyles on the ramparts; no one got near, no charges ever brought against him, so no justice would ever be done.

And anyone who turned informant would have a fate worse than death. That had been drummed into him even as a child. Fear. His whole life had been defined by it and he had gone on the run because of it.

The fear was real. No matter that he was thirty-five now. A widower. Had a multibillion-dollar-turnover business and a place on the *Forbes* list. It was still there, right down there on the streets of Manhattan, brewing. He could feel it. He could feel Arthur's wrath, could feel him coming for him.

Lauren had been the last one on the list to suffer the poison. He'd known as soon as he'd stepped out of his office and had seen her ashen face. At first he'd thought something had happened to Jacquelyn. Panic had grabbed his heart with both hands and squeezed the air from his lungs. Was that the moment he'd realised he loved her?

Lauren handed him the notepad where her shaky hand had written two sentences.

Daddy's home and he wants his money back.
Three p.m. Central Park West.

For a split second he thought about getting the jet ready, heading to Italy or London, anywhere but here. But there was iron in his blood now. There was lead in his spine. He could crush his fear, and he would not run any more. He would use every weapon he could and do the right thing.

Nikos gripped the barrier that encircled the top floor of his terrace and gazed at the park. Somewhere down there he was waiting. He and Bruno.

This was it. Time to finally grow up. He was not going to be the frightened boy hiding under his bedclothes any more. He was going to meet him here, get him to admit what he could with the police listening in, give him money if he had to and let the cops do the rest.

He was doing this for his mother, for Maria, but most of all for Jacquelyn. There would never be another chance, and there would definitely never be another Jacquelyn.

She was one in a million and worth every second of this. She was fighting for her business, her family, her reputation. She had more honesty and integrity than any other human being he had ever met, and she had stayed true to her principles until he had dragged her to his bed.

And he would never forgive himself for hurting her. She had trusted him and look what he had done. Trying to seduce her again and then sending her on her way because she wouldn't get into bed with him.

As soon as this was over he was going to find her. Maybe she would give him another chance. He put his hands together and bowed his head and prayed.

'Hello, Nikos. I'm… I'm outside with your father.'

The second she said the words, he grabbed the phone.

'You hear that. I've got your little friend. So let us up.'

Whatever Nikos said, Arthur's face lit up, then he nodded as the car moved forward like a tank, and then stopped at the carpet.

'This doesn't feel right,' said Bruno from the front.

'Relax. He'd never double-cross me. He hasn't got it in him. Here, sort yourself out,' he said, grabbing up her fallen shoes and bag and shoving them at her.

Jacquelyn slowly uncurled herself from the corner of the seat and tried to make her shaking limbs work. She stuffed her feet into the shoes, the pain of the blister not even registering as she forced her heels down and tried to smooth her dress with trembling hands.

The doorman seemed to hesitate before he stepped towards the vehicle.

'Right, Blondie, you're going to get out and smile at the nice man. Then walk inside. I'll be right beside you. And I don't need to tell you what will happen if you try anything stupid.'

The door opened. Sunlight danced on the green carpet. Her beige patent shoe struck the ground and she tried to stand, and round her waist the hateful hands of Nikos's father—a warning.

She climbed out and he came out right behind her, his hot breath at her ear, chilling and deadly. Bruno followed. She thought about running but her legs were useless, her mind was useless. All she could think about was Nikos and how he'd think she was part of this. How they might hurt him. What she could do to stop it happening.

The door to the building was opened, the concierge looked up and smiled, holding her eyes for an extra second, but then dipped her head back down to her screen.

Help! screamed Jacquelyn silently but there was nobody there to see the panic in her eyes.

The lift flew up, and bumped to a gentle halt at the penthouse. The doors slid open…

And there was Nikos and her heart soared. He looked right at her. His eyes telegraphed shock then anger in quick succession. She tried to mouth *It's OK* to him, but her lips wouldn't work. She felt a jab in her back, urging her forward.

'Long time no see,' sneered Arthur.

'This wasn't the deal,' he answered hoarsely.

'What…no hug for your old dad? After all this time?'

'Adding kidnapping to your list of crimes? I didn't think you'd be that stupid.'

'You can thank Bruno for that. He clocked her on the street. I hear she made quite an impression the first time they met—and here she is: the added insurance in case you decided to pretend you didn't know me again.'

He squeezed Jacquelyn's hand, making her shudder.

'Imagine being disowned by your own son. You'd think I brought him up better than that. All his fancy houses and cars and his money and no respect. What would you do with a son like that?'

Nikos stood still, eyes blazing furiously. Jacquelyn desperately wanted to run to him but she faltered, too afraid to move.

'You didn't bring me up. I owe everything

to my mother. You're no better than a cheap little drug dealer.'

'Your wife didn't mind that I was a dealer. Shame you didn't join the party. That was some party,' he said, turning to smile at Bruno.

'You low-life piece of scum. Just tell me what you want and get out of here.'

'You're the same scum as I am, underneath your suits and all your fancy stuff, you're still my son. You make money just like I make money. You get your needs met, you like your women…'

He trailed a finger down the back of Jacquelyn's arm and she shuddered and stiffened in one sickening moment.

Nikos opened his mouth and then closed it again. She saw a flicker pass over his eyes like an icy wind blowing through a stormy sky, but then his face was hard like granite.

'Come here, Jacquelyn.'

She heard the words, her heart flew to her chest and she leapt forward.

'Oh, no. Not so fast, *Jacquelyn.*'

Arthur's fingers curled round her upper arm, crushing it, but she didn't move or make a sound. She looked at Nikos, but the rage in his eyes chilled her and she looked away, too afraid to think of what he would do. It was like being between two bulls, their hooves stomping, breath thrusting from their noses, bull rings shining in the sun.

'Touch her and I swear I will rip your head off.'

Nikos stepped forward; he seemed to broaden, growing in stature, more terrifying by the moment. Jacquelyn sensed something weaken in Arthur behind her, and startled like a deer ready to run. At the same moment Nikos lunged for her, thrust his fist right past her head as he did so, bone meeting the flesh of Arthur's face and her body swung neatly behind his, shielded by him.

Arthur yelped in pain and stumbled off to the side, clutching his face.

'Bruno. Take care of this,' he said, through his hands cradling his head.

Bruno hesitated.

'We know the Feds are all over the Cayman investments. We'll settle for the Picasso.'

'You're getting nothing of mine.'

'Easy for you to say with all your millions. What do you think paid for the shirt on your back when you were a kid?'

'I'd rather have had nothing than anything involved in crime. You're the lowest of the low, making money from people who can't help themselves. Bullying the weak. I thank God every day that Mum got away from you.'

'She can't run far now though, can she?'

Loathing reared in Nikos like a monster and he lunged forward, trying to land another punch, but Bruno blocked his arm. Maddened, he swung again and shoved him crashing into one of the bronze art deco statues.

'Get out of my home. Get out before I rip your head off too.'

'Bruno. Get the painting…let's get out of here,' Arthur gasped.

Nikos lurched forward, heading straight for his father, who was now reeling, the bull finally charging the matador, the force of his movement huge and brutal and deadly.

And it broke Jacquelyn's heart to see him. This strong, gentle man, this man who had shown her such kindness, who had shown her how to make love and cherished her as much as his broken spirit could allow.

'No,' she called out and tried to pull him back. Her fingers landed on his back. 'Please don't be like him. You're better than that.'

Nikos stopped and reached for her, blindly grabbing at the air, as if he were stopping himself from falling off a cliff, and she found him and held him and hugged him close, pulling him back from the edge.

He looked into her eyes with such pain, and love. Just a moment, but it stretched there like a path to eternity and she knew she would go to the ends of the earth for this man.

'I'm sorry,' he whispered.

Then it all happened. Noises in the hallway, feet thundered on the parquet floor, the doors flew open, figures in dark uniforms. Guns.

Arthur roared, Nikos shielded her. Bruno stood, shoulders slumped, as if he had finally given in.

CHAPTER THIRTEEN

'So that is how I see us taking the intimate, highly personal experience that has been Ariana's trademark for generations, and translating it within each concession, and, even more importantly, online.'

Jacquelyn clicked the final slide on her deck and smiled round at the board. The faces were stony but she glanced up at Brody and saw him wink and give a discreet thumbs-up.

'Questions, anyone?' he said, as she sat beside him at the top of the table.

In the seconds that followed, Jacquelyn knew that her fate was being decided. Not just hers, but Victor's, the seamstresses' and machinists', her father's, her mother's. This was the deal of a lifetime and she had presented it with every ounce of skill she possessed.

'No questions. Just a guarantee of exclusivity. You come to us and you trade in the UK, but that's it.'

'If the price is right, yes,' said Jacquelyn, swinging her chair round slowly to face the CEO of Nikos's biggest rival. Her heart raced faster than the dollar signs she could see spinning in Brody's eyes. But she crossed her legs, steepled her fingers and kept her cool.

'And the stock is owned currently by whom?'

'I own ninety per cent and my business partner—' she nodded to Brody '—owns the other ten per cent.'

'Any plans for that to change? Or let me put it another way—any plans for Nikos Karellis to get involved?'

At the mention of Nikos's name, Jacquelyn's heart skipped a momentary beat. Brody opened his mouth to talk but she put her hand up, silencing him.

'I don't imagine anyone has asked you if your wife has bought stock recently, so you'll understand my surprise at your question.'

'House is our prime competitor. I have to ask.'

'My business affairs are wholly my own. As are my personal affairs.'

She stood up and the faces round the table all rose to watch her.

'If you feel that you need to know more than the quality of my work, or the health of my accounts, then perhaps our chemistry isn't going to work, after all.'

The room held its breath as she reached for her tablet and began to slide it into the leather pocket in her tote bag.

'Now, now, Miss Jones. Please don't be too hasty.'

She kept her eyes down but she could almost taste the buzz in the room.

'I think we're ready to make you an offer.'

She looked up into the eyes of every person round the table, checking for nodders or dissenters, and then, satisfied, she sat back in the sumptuous leather chair and smiled.

'Good. I'm ready to hear it,' she said.

Two hours later Jacquelyn stepped from her car onto the pavement outside her new favourite restaurant in Manhattan.

She stared up at the soaring glass and glimpses of bright blue sky above her head. She was completely in love with this city already, after only five days here. A city that welcomed, and spread out its possibilities like tempting canapés for her to try. Here, she *was* Ariana, unapologetically the CEO of a business that was contemporary and had legacy. She wasn't defined by her father or her grandmother, or by a failed relationship.

She was writing her own history one step at a time.

She stared in through the glass to see if she could see Nikos but the swirl of servers and lunchtime customers was too dense.

She stepped under the glass canopy just as she felt arms wrap around her.

'Nikos,' she sighed, sinking into his warm, strong body.

'Hello,' he said, tugging her towards him, and then he turned her slowly in his arms, and held her face. Then when he had smiled at her, and she had smiled at him, he kissed her slowly and thoroughly.

'I was beginning to think you'd stood me up. Where have you been?' he said, linking his fingers through hers and leading her off down the street.

'With my new best friends,' she said as they waited at the intersection to cross.

'Are you going to tell me who they are or do I have to guess?' said Nikos as he tucked his arm around her and walked them over the street.

'I'll give you a clue. They've got stores in every major city in northern USA and Australia. They've got an online platform to rival the best. And even better, they've just launched in China.'

'You signed with Blue?'

He stopped dead on the pavement, his hands

on her shoulders. She smiled so broadly it felt as if she'd run out of face.

'My biggest rival? You signed with my biggest rival?'

'It was beautiful, Nikos. They were looking for bespoke bridal. The store within the store. Ariana in Blue. Doesn't that just roll off the tongue? Authentic. Italian. They loved my new designs and they can give me the resources to scale everything up. And with the digital team that Brody has hired, we can convert the whole experience to the Internet too. Brides can upload their photos and measurements and we can dress the whole wedding party before they set a foot inside.'

'Wow,' he said as they started to walk again.

'But nothing will ever beat the personal touch. And that's what I'm going to get the most pleasure from creating. We're going to launch in Australia first.'

She'd kept that bit to the end, but he didn't pick up the cue.

'Jacquelyn, you're amazing. Look what you've done. In less than two weeks you've transformed your business. You've walked into New York and owned this city. You've gone further than I ever did.'

'Oh, come on, Nikos, you know that's not true. You built House from the dust.'

She threaded her fingers through his and stared happily at every passer-by, every shop window, every car.

'You and Mark are the only ones who truly know that. Everybody else thinks that I got it handed to me on a plate. But never mind me and House. Tell me how you handled the crusty old chief exec.'

Jacquelyn laughed and looked up. They were nearing the park. Their lunchtime place to stroll and talk, this past week.

'He asked about you.'

'What about me?' he said, pausing a moment to look at her. And just that sideways glimpse made her heart race. Those eyes that captured everything, those lips she ached to kiss, the inky trail of his tattoo snaking down under his Fifth Avenue shirt collar.

'He wanted to know if you would be getting involved further down the line.'

'And what did you tell him?'

'That it was none of his business. And if he wanted to make it his business then we wouldn't be taking this any further.'

They walked along together, her pointed patent toes and his black leather, totally in step. Bright sunshine bounced all around; they were nearing the park.

'*And* I pointed out that he wouldn't like it if I asked about his significant other.'

He was silent, but their feet stepped forward together, left, right, left, right, and she felt the press of his hip against hers, and the strength of his arm holding her close.

'Well. Good for you. Sounds like you handled the whole thing brilliantly. Brody is just as happy with the terms you got?'

She squeezed her arm against his side. Her little way of telling him to wind his jealous neck in.

'He's over the moon. Just like I am. I can go back to Lower Linton with my head held high. I can pay off all my debts and give everyone a pay rise. We can have our own Wellbeing Suite, and I can sponsor kids or start-ups, or do everything I ever dreamed of. Honestly, I've got everything now. And I can't thank you enough, Nikos. You were the first person I wanted to tell.'

'You've done it all yourself, Jacquelyn,' he said quietly. 'I just gave you a shove in the right direction.'

They were outside the gates of the park now, close to the Boathouse.

'So how do you want to celebrate?' he asked.

'This is all that I need,' she said simply, looking at the green water, the trees and paths, the people milling around. 'I don't need to drink champagne or eat a fancy dinner. I don't need any of that stuff. I've never been happier in my life.'

Nikos smiled at her, and trailed his fingers down her cheek. He was holding something back. She knew it. From the moment she'd met him she could tell he had something he wanted to say. She couldn't bear to get her hopes up though.

'How was your day? How did it go?'

'It's getting there,' he said, but there was exhaustion in his voice. 'I'm in the clear, but it'll take months to get through all the investigations and the court case. I'm going to be pretty tied up working with them for the next few weeks, but at least it feels as if we're getting somewhere.'

'And your mum? How is she?'

He bowed his head and when he looked up she could see the worry that leaked through at the mention of his mother.

'I need to take a trip out there next week.'

'Ah, yes, of course, I understand. I'm sure even if she doesn't seem to understand you, the universe will have a way of telling her that everything is going to be OK. That she's safe now. And that nobody else will suffer like she did.'

He tucked her close to his chest and breathed a deep, soulful breath. Under her cheek, his heart pounded a strong, slow beat, a sound she relished, more than any other.

'You're a sweet, wonderful woman, Jacquelyn. You say exactly the right things. I wish she could have met you. I'd love for you two to get to know one another.'

They were right at the Boathouse now. He'd led them into the queue for a rowing boat. Then they were stepping into a boat, steadying and balancing as Nikos took the oars and paddled them out through the smooth green water.

'I should visit my own parents,' she said, enjoying the slow steady glide and the sound of the oars slipping through the water. 'It's been such a long time since I saw them. And now I've got something amazing to tell them, I really want to do it in person.'

Nikos nodded slowly as he rowed them further out, the heavy canopy of the trees screening them from the world.

'Yep. We need to look after our folks. What goes around, comes around.'

She sat back, watching his muscles flex and extend under the sheen of his shirt. There was nowhere more romantic in the whole of Manhattan. There was no one she would rather be with.

'Where are we going?' she asked.

He looked behind.

'Oh, not much further.'

Her heart was beginning to thunder in her chest.

He smiled and winked, and she smiled back. Tears began to form in her eyes, but she mustn't, she mustn't let herself believe it until it was true. They'd never spoken again about marriage, he hadn't pressed her to sleep with him and she'd spent every night in her own suite at the hotel, awake or asleep, dreaming of Nikos.

But it swirled around them. Those unsaid words, their deep desires. She felt her love for him so strongly, but he'd been resolutely silent, occupied completely by his father's arrest and the investigations.

She looked at him now, his dark head bent to check if anyone was close by, then a smile flashed over his lips as there, in the centre of the pond he tucked the oars up into the boat.

They drifted for a moment, caught in each other's eyes.

'Are you happy, Jacquelyn?' he said, smiling softly.

She felt her lip tremble. She nodded, unable to speak.

'Is there anything that would make you even happier?'

She swallowed, she opened her mouth, but no words could come out. She felt her face pucker up with tears of joy, ready to be shed.

'If I told you that I can't live without you, would that make you happy?'

She sat up straight in the little boat, perched on the edge of the little seat, her eyes fixed on his as he reached into the pocket of his trousers.

'Because it's true. I can't. I don't want to. I want you in my life. I didn't think I would ever say these words, but I didn't know love until I knew you, and that's the truth.'

'I want you in mine too, for ever,' she whispered. And the hugeness of what she had just said struck her. She meant for ever and ever.

'For the rest of our lives,' said Nikos and she nodded because it was true. 'So that means getting married. I know how much it means to you, and there's nothing I ever want to deny you.'

'It's meant to be, Nikos.'

He held her close.

'I know. I know you understand it, and you understand me. There's no one else for me and there never will be. So let's get married. For love. For ever. For the children we'll have and the love we'll show them.'

He opened his fist and there was a small

blue velvet box. She clasped her hands and he opened it. And there inside was the most beautiful ring she had ever seen. It had one large, brilliant diamond and two smaller ones at either side set on a slim gold band. It sparkled in the sunlight, as he lifted it carefully from its velvet nest.

As if they had practised a thousand times, she extended her hand into his and he lifted it and kissed it.

'Will you marry me, Jacquelyn? Will you make me the happiest man alive?' he said, holding her hand and sliding the ring down to rest in its new home.

And then she nodded, and he kissed her.

There were no words, there were just the two lovers drifting in a boat on the lake in Central Park, lost in each other's arms, each other's kisses and each other's dreams.

EPILOGUE

Sᴜɴsᴇᴛ ʙᴀᴛʜᴇᴅ ᴀ gentle pastel palette over the terracotta roofs and whitewashed walls of the village. Shades of lilac, peach and pink lay in overlapping bands of colour from sky to horizon to sea. In the warm evening air, a swoop of swallows darted here and there, looking for insects, before resting in the villa's eaves in their tiny muddy nests.

Jacquelyn watched from the guest bedroom, as she had watched every sunset for the past week. It lifted her heart to see them, and all the other flora and fauna of this beautiful island, things one could only see standing patiently still and quiet. It was a tonic, after New York and everything that had happened. The frantic bustle of the city, the arrests of Arthur and Bruno, the newly launched Ariana in Blue.

Standing here now, staring at the slow, peaceful world falling asleep every night, she knew that this was all that really mattered, the movement of the earth and nature upon it, this little island and its people, the birds and the flowers, and the man who had laid it all at her feet.

She stepped forward onto the terrace and breathed deeply, feeling a smile gild her face. She was so lucky, so happy, so astonished that she was here at all, about to take the next steps in her life. Ariana was safe, probably for ever. Her parents could live out their lives in Spain. She had sewn everything up as neatly as the stitches on the wedding dress that now hung in the next room, the dress she would wear tomorrow.

A knock sounded at the door.

'Can I come in?'

She turned, the smile expanding into a grin at the sound of Nikos's voice, and then as he walked into the room she ran into his open arms, burying herself in his chest, holding on and absorbing him without the slightest shame.

'Everybody is settled in their suites and your mum seems to have stopped crying for the time being.'

'She's so happy for me, everyone is.' She sighed as he swung her gently backwards and forward. 'But I'm going to miss you again to-night.'

'You know where I'll be. Just along the hall-way,' he said, with a smile in his voice. 'You wouldn't get lost.'

'I know, I know,' she said. 'But it's only one more night.'

'And then our wedding, finally,' he said, smiling.

'We've got our whole lives ahead, Nikos. Nothing but these beautiful skies and whatever we want to do, underneath them.'

He nodded.

'I only wish Mum could have made it here. It would have made her so happy.'

A tiny tear sprang into his eye and he tight-ened his jaw, holding himself in check. She wished he would let it go, but he'd been res-olutely strong through it all and there would be more to come. She would do everything to help him heal. Everything.

She touched his cheek, feeling the rough stubble under her palm, the bone of his jaw and cheek, hard and yielding as he was himself.

'She's in a happier place now, Nikos. No more suffering.'

He closed his eyes, and tried to smile, but she knew now of the pain that had risen to the sur-face. It broke her heart to think of anyone liv-ing as he had lived, watching his mother beaten, running away and then learning that she had been so badly injured she had nearly died.

What guilt he carried. And none of it deserved.

'You're an amazing woman, Jacquelyn. I never thought I would find anyone like you.'

She nodded and smoothed her hands over his solid, strong back. Her silence said everything. The past was the past…those ghosts didn't matter any more. This was real, because she knew she would do anything for Nikos, and he her. It felt that the world was safe now; no matter what, they would be there for each other.

'We've found each other, Nikos. We were always going to happen. We just didn't know how or when or where.'

'And tomorrow we make it legal.'

She nodded as the tears now filled her own eyes.

'Tomorrow I finally see the dress I inspired. How many men can say that they inspired a collection of wedding dresses?'

'Sex out of wedlock has its advantages. But you'll never get me to admit it in public.'

'All I want you to admit is that you'll be my wife. In Agios Stephanos in front of your family and my friends. And I promise I'll make a polite, respectful speech about the night we met. And the night after that…'

'You won't whisper a word about the night after that.' She laughed, punching his rock-hard abs. 'I'd never live it down! A woman with my reputation, for goodness' sake.'

He stretched out his arms, and stared down at her, and the love that was in his eyes turned fiery and flames of desire lit all over her body.

'And then?' she whispered.

'And then we'll dance our first dance.'

'And I'll throw my bouquet.'

'And *then*…?'

She breathed in deeply, her chest rising and falling, thinking of the pleasure they had already shared and the pleasure they would share for evermore. How could life ever be any better than that?

'Then we'll make love. Husband and wife.'

'And live happily ever after.'

He kissed her lips, and held her close for the final time.

'Goodnight, Miss Jones,' he said, and she turned to see him standing in the doorway, his handsome silhouette outlined in the lamplight. 'Sleep well. I'll see you tomorrow.'

'Goodnight, Nikos,' she said.

She closed the door and walked to the dressing room, where her white dress shimmered and danced in the moonlight. And she wept tears of joy, knowing that tomorrow she would wear her beautiful dress to be married to the man she truly loved.

* * * * *

If you enjoyed
Redeemed by Her Innocence,
you're sure to enjoy these other stories
by Bella Frances!

The Argentinian's Virgin Conquest
The Italian's Vengeful Seduction
The Consequence She Cannot Deny
The Tycoon's Shock Heir

Available now!